**"That does it, Kel, no more *UFO Today* for you," Kenan said sternly.**

Kel tried to protest, but Kenan quickly cut him off.

"Nah, I'm serious." He began flipping through the magazine, yelling out story items at random. "No more 'My Baby's from Outer Space.' "

"But—"

"No more 'My Vacation on Venus!' "

"But—"

"No more 'Five-Thousand-Dollar Reward for Photos of Alien Life.' "

"But—"

"Five thousand dollars for one picture?" Kenan peered at the article closer to make sure he wasn't reading it wrong. He wasn't.

A small smile stole its way across Kenan's face. Then, as he rubbed his hands together thoughtfully in front of him, it grew into a big smile, which soon turned itself into a devious, gleaming, scheming sort of grin.

Kel knew that look. He had seen it a lot. And it always meant one thing.

"Kenan, what's that look for?" His voice shook nervously because he already knew the answer.

"Because, Kel," Kenan answered, "I've got a plan."

**Kenan & Kel™ books:**

Aw, Here It Goes!
Family and Food and Orange Soda
ALIENS

**Look for these other Nickelodeon® books:**

Good Burger™
Good Burger™ 2 Go
All That™: Fresh Out the Box

Available from POCKET Books

For orders other than by individual consumers, Pocket Books grants a discount on the purchase of **10 or more** copies of single titles for special markets or premium use. For further details, please write to the Vice President of Special Markets, Pocket Books, 1230 Avenue of the Americas, 9th Floor, New York, NY 10020-1586.

For information on how individual consumers can place orders, please write to Mail Order Department, Simon & Schuster Inc., 100 Front Street, Riverside, NJ 08075.

# ALIENS

Steve Holland

AN ARCHWAY PAPERBACK
Published by POCKET BOOKS
New York London Toronto Sydney Singapore

The sale of this book without its cover is unauthorized. If you purchased this book without a cover, you should be aware that it was reported to the publisher as "unsold and destroyed." Neither the author nor the publisher has received payment for the sale of this "stripped book."

This book is a work of fiction. Names, characters, places and incidents are products of the author's imagination or are used fictitiously. Any resemblance to actual events or locales or persons, living or dead, is entirely coincidental.

AN ARCHWAY PAPERBACK *Original*

An Archway Paperback published by
POCKET BOOKS, a division of Simon & Schuster Inc.
1230 Avenue of the Americas, New York, NY 10020

Copyright © 1999 by Viacom International Inc. All rights reserved.
Based on the Nickelodeon series entitled "Kenan & Kel."

All rights reserved, including the right to reproduce
this book or portions thereof in any form whatsoever.
For information address Pocket Books, 1230 Avenue
of the Americas, New York, NY 10020

ISBN: 0-671-03431-6

First Archway Paperback printing March 1999

10 9 8 7 6 5 4 3

NICKELODEON, Kenan & Kel, and all related titles, logos and characters are trademarks of Viacom International Inc.

AN ARCHWAY PAPERBACK and colophon are registered trademarks of Simon & Schuster Inc.

Cover photography by Blake Little

Printed in the U.S.A.

IL. 5+

For Ellis

# OPEN

"Hey everybody and welcome to another exciting Kenan and Kel adventure. I am often called Kenan!"

"Uh . . . Kenan? Who are you talking to? There's no one there."

"Yes there is, Kel! I'm talking to all of the people who are reading this book right now. Look, there, right up there."

"Ohhhhh, hey. Look at you all. Hey! You! Yeah, you! Why don't you put a shirt on while you read our book? Man, I don't want to have to look at that all day."

"Kel, leave the kid alone. It's okay, wear whatever you want."

"Whoa! Whoa! Slow down, you don't have to read that fast. It's a whole lot more fun if you read it really slow. Maybe you want to go ahead and act it out to yourself. Just make sure no one's looking first or they're gonna think that you're a little weird."

"Thank you for that wonderful tip, Kel."

"No problem."

"Hey Kel, have you ever stared up into the sky at night and wondered if there was anything out there?"

"You mean like orange soda?"

"Nah, fruit bat! I wasn't talking about orange soda."

"But, Kenan, I love orange soda!"

"I know that you do. Everybody knows that you do. But I was talking about something else. I was talking about life on other planets, you know aliens and stuff."

"Ohhhhhhhh! Hey Kenan, do you think that if there is life on other planets that they drink orange soda?"

"I don't know, Kel. But maybe you'll get the chance to ask them yourself before this book is over. Now come on, spacey!"

"Kenan? Who will I get to ask? Kenan!? Does that mean that we get to drink a lot of orange soda in this book? Kenan? Why can't you ever just come out and tell me what's going to happen? Awwwww, here it goes!!"

# CHAPTER ONE

A shiny round metal object drifted lazily down through the cloudless blue sky. It slowed to a gentle stop in midair and floated, hovering in place over the peaceful town below. The object looked a lot like a giant, floating hubcap. Except that, unlike most hubcaps, it was fitted with a large, deadly-looking laser gun on its gleaming metallic surface. Also, unlike most other hubcaps, it was not from the tire of a nearby car, but from another galaxy a billion light-years away. That's right, this was no ordinary hubcap. This was a flying saucer. Something about its saucer shape and the way it flew gave it away.

Deep inside the extraterrestrial bowels of the ship sat a vile, slimy tentacled being that would never, ever be mistaken for a hubcap. He was the evil alien commander, Bob. And there was only one thing on his evil alien mind. The destruction of the earth! Slime oozed from the wrinkly folds where his face would have been if he had a face. He raised all twenty of his slimy purple tentacles dramatically in the air and in his bizarrely sweet, chirping voice, he gave the command.

The deadly laser rotated in its turret. It stopped with a loud, metallic clang as it locked in on its target, a small, sleepy suburb of Chicago that seemed to have no idea that it was about to be blasted into a million small and sleepy bits by an unidentified flying hubcap from another world.

Commander Bob oozed a particularly gleeful trail of slime down his not-quite-a-chin and chirped two short whistles and a lovely high-pitched caw which, translated into English, meant "Fire the deadly laser beam at the unsuspecting town below . . . please." For an evil alien commander, he was very polite. Several equally slimy, equally purple aliens erupted into a bustle of activity at their commander's orders. They pushed several brightly colored buttons with several of their brightly colored tentacles. A low hum began to emanate from the laser as it warmed up to fire.

Suddenly, a shot burst from out of nowhere and smashed into the ship, shaking it violently to the side. Smoke belched from the brand-new twisted hole that had just been torn into the ship's shiny metallic side. The saucer wobbled, bobbled, then, in a way very few hubcaps ever do, it exploded into fiery little pieces of alien metal and crashed to the ground.

"I did it! I did it!" shrieked Kel as he jumped up and down in a victorious dance of joy. "I blew up the alien mother ship. I am the Alien Attack champion of the world!" A computer graphic flashed on the screen of the video game confirming Kel's boast. It read "Alien

Commander, Bob, Destroyed! You are the Alien Attack Champion of the World."

Video Schmideo was the coolest arcade in Chicago. It was famous for three reasons. First, its glowing neon sign, which stood a staggering thirty feet off the roof of the building, was not only the largest sign for a video arcade in Chicago, but also happened to be one of the largest freestanding eyesores anywhere in the country.

Second, Video Schmideo boasted the most amazing collection of video games this side of Video Heaven. (Video Heaven, of course, was a rival arcade several blocks down the street.) From the moment you entered, your ears were assaulted with the pumped-up beeping, whirring, exploding sounds of video fun. All over the place kids were videofishing, videowrestling; even the indescribably disgusting videobelching machine, which re-created the experience of an actual burp right down to the taste and smell for only a quarter, was usually occupied.

The third and perhaps most important reason that Video Schmideo had won the coveted title of "Best Video Arcade on the Face of the Planet" a whopping seven years in a row was its food. It wasn't particularly great food. It wasn't even particularly good food. In fact some would argue that it hardly qualified as food at all. It was, just like it said on the towering, radiant neon monstrosity out front, Pizza on a Stick!

"I did it! I won!" Kel repeated as a huge victorious smile spread across his narrow face, revealing the small gap that nestled comfortably in between his two front teeth. His eyes glowed with pride as he wrapped his arms around the video game machine, puckered up, and planted a big smooch right on the screen! The game didn't seem to mind, and somehow went on about its business of beeping and whirring, throwing in the occasional rumble or explosion for good measure, as if nothing out of the ordinary was happening. Kenan didn't seem quite as calm.

"Awwww, nasty. Get your lips off of that machine. You don't know where that's been," he said, a little disgusted at where Kel had chosen to plant his lips. Kenan Rockmore was Kel's best friend and had been since they were five. That meant that Kenan was quite used to saying things like "Kel, get your lips off of that machine!" or "Kel, soda is not a fruit." Or his personal favorite: "No, Kel, there are no little men living in your nose." Kenan didn't really mind saying those things; after all, Kel was his best friend. The fact that Kel was a little . . . different than other people was part of the reason they got along so well. Besides, who else could Kenan talk into following along with all of his crazy dreams and schemes.

Several customers stopped to stare as Kel pressed his face more firmly against the stand-up video game and began to make loud, wet smooching noises.

Kenan turned towards the staring customers with an apologetic sort of glance. "Oh . . . uh . . . see, he just, you know, dropped his gum on that game"—he stumbled through an explanation, making it up as he went—"and now he's . . . just trying to get it back . . . with his mouth. See? Heh-heh." Kenan quickly whirled back to face Kel, running his hands impatiently through the short, stubby dreadlocks that pointed up off of his head in all directions. "Kel, would you stop smooching with that machine. People are staring at you. And besides it's weird." Kenan glanced at his watch casually. It was 12:50 P.M. on Saturday afternoon. Kenan lowered his arm, then suddenly stopped and jerked his arm back up to his face to glance at his watch again, a little less casually this time. Twelve fifty?! He was supposed to be at work at one o'clock. "Late for work! Aw, I'm late for work. Come on, Kel, let's go!" His foot began impatiently tapping on the sticky floor of the arcade.

Kel removed his lips from the game, leaving a smudged imprint of his kisser smeared across the glass.

"Hey Kenan," he inquired innocently, "can I borrow another quarter?"

"No!" Kenan snapped. "You've been borrowing quarters off of me all day. Besides, we've got to go. You can not borrow a quarter."

"All right, fine. Can I borrow a hundred bucks then?"

Kenan stared at Kel. "If I wouldn't loan you a quarter, then why would you think I would loan you a hundred bucks?"

"I thought that maybe you didn't have a quarter."

Kenan's eyes squinted up, and he shook his head from side to side in frustration. Kel's logic often had this effect on him. "Would you just come on? I'm gonna be late for work; we gotta go."

Kel was about to agree when suddenly he stopped. There was something in the air. A scent of some sort. He sniffed, flaring his nostrils in the direction of the smell. It was something familiar. Something hot and greasy and on a stick. He tilted his head back and inhaled more sharply, drawing the scent far up into his nose. "Pizza on a Stick!" he bellowed, throwing his hands up above his head in a wild display of excitement and joy. His nostrils flared wildly at the sheer sensory excitement that they had just experienced. Then, as if drawn by a very large, very powerful magnet, Kel turned and bolted for the concession counter, leaving Kenan standing alone beside the warm glow of video alien death.

"Awwww, man!" Kenan groaned as he glanced at his watch. "Twelve fifty-two. Gonna be late . . . gonna be late, and it's all Kel's fault!" he muttered to himself as he trudged off after Kel.

"Hi and thanks for choosing Video Schmideo would you like to try our Pizza on a Stick?" The employee's squelching nasal voice cracked as his tongue raced toward the end of the sentence, blurring the words together into one long verbal mush.

Kel had no idea what the employee had just said to him and, quite frankly, he didn't care. He was on a mission. "No thanks, I just want a Pizza on a Stick."

"That'swhatIsaid," the employee spat out in one quick, mashed-up ball of words. Sweat began to break out underneath the tall black-and-orange–striped hat that perched precariously at the top of his long, pointy head. Even though the rest of the arcade was air-conditioned to arctic perfection, the air around the concession stand was warm and heavy with the promise of piping hot Italian food, skewered on a wooden stick.

"Yeah, uh . . . that's great, you know, whatever it

was that you said and all," Kel replied, trying to be nice, "but I just want a Pizza on a Stick." He began dancing back and forth from one foot to the other in food-expectant delirium.

The employee sighed and wondered briefly to himself why no one ever listened to him. He wiped his brow with the back of his hand, breathed in deeply, and then, in a furious sprint of words, blurted out, "Fine, coming-rightup!" His voice cracked, making the end of the sentence come out in a grating high-pitched screech. He was not at all pleasant to listen to and was almost never asked to sing at parties.

Kenan marched up to the front of the line where his friend waited. He grabbed him by the shoulder, spun him around, and eyed him up and down, from his purple tennis shoes to the matching hat that was pulled snugly over his head. His plaid shirt hung open over the black T-shirt that he wore underneath. "Didn't you hear me say that I was late for work?" An edge of frustration crept into Kenan's voice.

Kel looked at Kenan as if he had just asked the dumbest question ever. "Of course I did, Kenan. I'm not deaf. Sheesh." He shook his head patronizingly. "I just came to get a Pizza on a Stick before we left."

A thought struck Kenan. "Kel, I thought you didn't have any money."

"Why would you think that?"

"Because you've been borrowing quarters from me all day!" Kenan eyed his friend sternly, waiting for an explanation.

"I was only borrowing quarters from you because I

didn't want to waste my own money playing Alien Attack," Kel answered calmly just as the long-faced employee handed him his Pizza on a Stick.

Pizza on a Stick was not just a clever name for a food. It pretty much described exactly what you were about to eat. A normal triangular slice of pizza that had been run through from flat, doughy crust to pointy tip with a wooden stick. The stick itself served no real purpose. In fact, it actually made eating the pizza more difficult. But some clever marketing executive, working late at night on obviously little sleep, had determined that people loved food on a stick. And after several failed attempts at marketing such clever creations as Liver on a Stick and the hugely disastrous Spaghetti on a Stick, he finally hit gold with Pizza. The only actual benefit of the stick was that it prevented you from burning your hands on what was usually a way-hotter-than-average slice of pizza.

Kel grabbed the pizza joyfully; his eyes widened with hunger; his taste buds stood proudly in his mouth, waiting for the happy moment when pizza would meet tongue. Cheese dripped its way down the crust as steam rose from the pierced, triangular slab of pie. Kel drew it slowly towards his mouth, savoring the smell of the freshly baked food as it neared the end of its journey to his belly.

Kenan's finger shot tentatively into the air. "Kel, I think you might want to let that cool down for a second, it looks really . . ." Before Kenan could utter the word hot, something very bad happened. Kel took a bite of the pizza.

There are many varying degrees of heat that are

known to humankind. A hot summer's day may register at about one hundred and five degrees Fahrenheit, while lava that spews from a volcano, instantly devouring everything in its path with its blazing molten fury, would come in at several million degrees Fahrenheit. The pizza that Kel put into his mouth fell somewhere closer to the lava end of the scale.

Steam shot out of Kel's nostrils. His usually brown skin turned an altogether hotter shade of red. Inside his mouth, there was a taste bud riot. The roof of his mouth liquefied, boiled, and became one with the searing molten cheese that flowed under it. Tiny pain receptors practically fell over each other in their demented race to reach his brain, each carrying the same message.

"HOTTTTTT!" Kel shrieked painfully. All activity in the arcade stopped as every eye riveted on the shrieking Kel. He screamed again, a loud burning bellow. Smoke poured from his lips as he ran around the crowded room, fanning his hand wildly in front of his melting mouth.

Kenan had to think quick. He grabbed a soda out of a nearby kid's hands, ran up to Kel, and threw the liquid right at him. Unfortunately, Kenan's timing was a little off and he ended up throwing the soda into the space where Kel had been just a second before. What was now standing in that space was the large glowing Alien Attack game that really had no desire to be covered in soda. The soda, not seeming to care one bit about what the video game wanted or didn't want, doused it anyway with a sticky wet sploosh.

"This can't be good," Kenan muttered to himself as

he scrunched his face up in preparation for the bad things to come.

For a second the machine seemed to be okay. It was beeping and whirring and smoking just like normal. *Huh, that's odd,* thought Kenan, *I don't remember the game smoking.* Just about the time that thought was making its way through Kenan's clenched and panicked brain, the usual whirring and bleeping of the game started to give way to an altogether more unpleasant crackling, snapping sound. Sparks shot out of the plastic casing of the machine, showering the room with a bright spray of electricity. The crowd that had gathered to watch slowly backed away as the machine began to rumble. The smoke that had been drifting lightly now began to pour heavily out of the game. Then, with a final sputtering, coughing hack, the game died. Even Kel took time out from his burning mouth to stop and notice what had happened.

"Kenan, you killed Alien Attack!"

The sidewalk that ran underneath Video Schmideo's towering neon sign was not at all unusual. It was white, like other sidewalks. It was concrete, just like other sidewalks. And, exactly like other sidewalks, it was terribly uncomfortable to land on. Which is why Kenan and Kel sounded so uncomfortable two minutes later when they landed on it with loud, heavy thuds.

"And stay out!" shouted the large, burly bouncer who had been kind enough to toss them out of the arcade and onto the very uncomfortable, very concrete sidewalk outside.

Kenan lay there for just a moment wondering silently

why these things always seemed to happen to him. Kel quickly untangled himself from Kenan's limbs and jumped to his feet.

"Oh yeah," he shouted at the bouncer who still stood blocking the doorway with his thick tree-trunk of a body. "Well, see if we ever come back to your arcade again, buddy!"

"Uh, Kel, I kinda think that that's the idea," Kenan tried to explain as he slowly pulled himself to his feet, brushing the dirt from his clothes.

"Well, that's rude," Kel exclaimed.

"We blew up their video game." Kenan spelled it out slowly for his friend; sometimes that was the only way.

Kel thought about it for just a moment, then his face lit up as a wave of understanding washed over him. "Ohhhhhh." He looked up at the bouncer with a slightly embarrassed glance. "Sorry."

# CHAPTER TWO

Chris Potter would never be mistaken for a secret agent, with his long thin face, prominent nose, and the brown helmet of hair that had been sprayed into a hard protective shell on top of his head. Even his chin looked as though it wanted to be a little farther away from the rest of his face than it actually was. Chris was nothing like a secret agent. Secret agents were suave and cool and dangerous and almost never lived with their mothers. Chris, on the other hand, was a grocer. He wore an apron, and he had lived with his mother for thirty years. No, Chris would probably never get sent halfway across the world on some top secret government assignment with the fate of the planet resting in his hands. But that suited Chris just fine. Traveling always made his allergies act up anyway. And besides, if he was off saving the world, who would take care of Mother? Chris was content being a grocer.

He paced back and forth across the small, squarish floor of Rigby's Grocery, which he owned. Rigby's was not a big store, nor was it a terribly pretty store. It was, in all respects, a very average little store. Surprisingly, business had been good enough that a couple of years ago Chris had hired a little extra help.

Right now, like many days since, Chris was wondering exactly where that extra help was and why it was over twenty minutes late.

He paced the length of the store again, making his way from the small dairy display near the door, past the squat wooden apple bin, and all the way over to the soda cooler which stood against the far wall right in between the cluttered magazine rack and the lone checkout counter.

He turned to gaze up at the clock which hung just above Rigby's small deli counter, which was filled to the brim with ham, turkey, and a surprisingly large supply of head cheese. *One twenty-two. Where could Kenan be?* he thought to himself. He paced across the store, turned, marched back, and looked at the clock again. "One twenty-two and ten seconds. If he doesn't get here soon, I'm going to be late picking Mother up from her sumo wrestling class." Chris's stomach clenched up into a tight little ball at the thought. Mother didn't like it when he was late picking her up. And Chris had learned long ago that it wasn't wise to upset Mother.

He fiddled nervously with his trusty blue apron. *Where could he be?*

"Man, you should have seen your face when you bit into that Pizza on a Stick. Boy, that was funny." Kenan bulged his eyes out and fanned ridiculously at his mouth in a goofy exaggerated impression of Kel. Both of them cracked up, laughing out loud as they strolled down the quiet tree-lined street that led towards Rigby's.

Kel wrestled his laughter under control as the pain in his mouth subsided in the cool air. "Yeah, but that wasn't as funny as when you poured motor oil all over your head and then started jumping up and down on one foot, clucking like a parrot." Kel clutched his sides as another wave of laughter burst up from his belly at the memory.

Kenan shot Kel an amused look. It was a look he gave a lot. "What? Kel, that never happened."

Kel thought about it for a second as his laughter subsided. "Oh, yeah. I must have made that up." He shrugged nonchalantly.

Kenan shook his head and grinned to himself. Kel was always saying stuff that made Kenan shake his head and grin. It was one of the reasons that he liked hanging out with him. He never knew what Kel was going to say next. Probably because Kel never knew what he was going to say next. He just said whatever popped into his head. He never worried whether it was going to come out sounding weird or goofy. As a result, a lot of what Kel said came out sounding weird or goofy, oftentimes both.

"Well, it's about time," Chris bellowed angrily as soon as Kenan stepped foot inside the store.

"It's about what time?" Kel asked as he casually pushed his way past Kenan and made a speedy beeline for the orange-soda cooler. He hoped that Chris meant it was about time to drink orange soda. Then, he decided that even if that's not what Chris had meant, it was still a really good idea. He grabbed a bottle of orange soda from the cooler and began drinking.

Kel loved to drink orange soda. It was his very favorite thing in the whole world. In fact, the only thing he liked better than drinking orange soda was pouring orange soda over his head and dancing around in it. But since some people seemed to find that a little odd and disturbing, he rarely got the chance to do it.

"It's about time that you got to work!" Chris continued, trying to sound as angry and unhappy as he could. He had recently been listening to a series of cassettes in his car which were titled "How to Be a Better Boss and Not Be Such a Wimp All the Time." One thing the tapes seemed to stress over and over was the importance of sounding angry and unhappy when one of your employees showed up late.

He squinted angrily at Kenan in a very "I'm disappointed in you" sort of way. "I'm supposed to pick up Mother from her sumo wrestling class in fifteen minutes and you're making me late!" Chris barked. He started wringing his hands nervously as he thought of Mother sitting outside of class, having to chat with strange sumo wrestlers as she desperately wondered why her only son wasn't around to pick her up on time.

"Sumo wrestling? Well isn't your mom feisty," Kenan said as he watched his boss nervously pat down the brown helmet of hair that sat on top of his head.

Chris didn't have time for this. He had to leave to pick up Mother. But first he had to say something very tough and bosslike. Something that would let Kenan know how angry and disappointed he was. The tapes were very firm about letting your employees know how angry and disappointed you were in them.

"Just get to work; I'll be back later" was all he could come up with. Then, he quickly pulled the blue Rigby's apron off over his head and rushed out of the door.

"Sumo wrestling?" Kenan said again to himself to see if it sounded any less strange this time. Nope, just as strange.

As Kel shook the last of the sweet orangy beverage from the bottle and down his welcoming throat, a thought suddenly occurred to him. An utterly disturbing sort of thought. The kind of thought that would keep him up late at night, or at the very least give him nightmares or maybe some bad indigestion. "Kenan, if we're not allowed to go back into Video Schmideo again, then where am I going to get to play Alien Attack?"

Kenan was only half paying attention as he readied himself for work. "I don't know," he offered. "A different arcade." He pulled an apron on, walked over to an open box that lay just underneath the canned-goods shelf, and started pulling out cans of "I Can't Believe It's Not Beef" and stocking them on the shelf.

Kenan's answer didn't seem to calm the disturbing feeling that had gripped Kel by the large intestine and had now begun to squeeze. "Another arcade? But what if they don't have Alien Attack at another arcade. Then I'll never be able to play it again."

"Good," Kenan muttered. "It was getting too expensive for me anyway."

Kel rushed over and yanked Kenan to his feet in a panic. He found a handful of Kenan's apron, clutched it, and shook him back and forth as he spoke. "But you don't understand, Kenan. If I can't play Alien Attack then I won't be prepared to save the earth when the aliens invade for real! Ohhh, the earth is gonna be overtaken by evil, slimy beings from another planet all because my Pizza on a Stick was too hot. Ohhh, the evil workings of fate have doomed us all!" Kel's face flushed a bright shade of red from the effort of both yelling and shaking at the same time. It was quite a workout, and he soon realized that he couldn't keep both of them up for long.

His hands slowly released their viselike grip on Kenan and slipped to his sides. Now that he was no longer physically shaking anyone back and forth, Kel reasoned, he should be able to yell in desperation a little while longer. "What are we gonna do? Ahhhhh, what are we gonna do?" He slid down to the floor and cradled the box full of "I Can't Believe It's Not Beef" in his trembling arms.

"Well," Kenan started, a little flustered by his friend's sudden outburst. It was another in a long line of things that Kenan hadn't expected to happen today. "First, I think we ought to get you the psychiatric help that you apparently need. And then you should probably tell me . . . WHAT THE HECK YOU'RE TALKING ABOUT!!" Kenan shouted the last bit partly for effect, but mostly because he truly had no idea what Kel was talking about.

Kel was no longer upset. He had passed that stage and had quickly moved on to the stage where he resigned himself to the fact that aliens were going to take over the earth and turn all the humans into house pets. He sighed deeply and offered a look of pity to Kenan. *Poor guy,* he thought. *He has no idea what's going on.* Slowly, Kel pulled himself to his feet and began to explain.

"You see, Kenan"—he placed a hand on his friend's shoulder for moral support—"aliens are coming to take over the earth and turn all of us humans into house pets." He spoke as calmly and soothingly as possible, as if talking to a small child. After all, this was big news and he didn't want to panic Kenan any more than necessary. "In fact," he continued, "they're already living among us while they prepare for the attack. But we can't tell because they look just like you and me. See, aliens are crafty like that."

Kenan knocked Kel's hand off of his shoulder with an annoyed smack. He had heard enough of his friend's crazy talk. Kel couldn't really believe in aliens. People who believed in aliens were weird and Kel was . . . Okay, maybe he could believe. "Man, where do you get that garbage from? There are no such things as aliens." He snorted a short little reproachful sort of snort, then added to himself, "Aliens. Shoot."

Kel was not going to give up that easily. Kenan was his friend and he deserved to know the truth. He rushed over to the magazine rack and quickly shuffled through glossy-covered copies of *Sissy* and *Lady Land,* carelessly tossing them onto the floor as he continued his frantic search until, finally, way in the back, hidden behind the last copy of *Dirt Digest,* he found what he was looking for.

*UFO Today* was not a very popular magazine. In fact, it was probably only slightly more popular than the amazingly poor-selling *Castor Oil Weekly*. The reason that it managed to sell slightly better than that oil-related periodical was that *UFO Today*'s stories never lasted longer than it would take to read during a really quick trip to the bathroom, and more importantly, it contained lots and lots of pictures.

Kel shoved the glossy colorful copy of *UFO Today* into Kenan's hands. "See Kenan, it's all right here in this magazine." Kenan sighed, shook his head, then grudgingly peered down at the magazine.

On the bright cover was the headline, in large friendly letters, "Alien Invasion Imminent." Directly underneath the eye-catching lettering was a large, colorful photo of a very attractive girl who seemed to be terribly afraid of the frightening green-headed mutant alien that was looming over her, clutching some sort of hi-tech–looking alien death ray in its cowlike hoof. Underneath the photo in tiny block lettering was the disclaimer, "This photo is a reenactment of what an alien invasion may look like. It is not an actual photo of actual aliens. Please don't sue."

"Yeah, right," Kenan muttered. "Kel, this stuff isn't real, it's all just made up. There are no such thing as aliens."

"Yes there are. You just can't tell because they go around looking normal and stuff. But look, this magazine tells you how to spot them. Check it out." Kel grabbed the magazine from Kenan and quickly thumbed through it. He flipped past the article titled "Martian Madness," didn't even glance at the exposé "Men Are from Earth, Aliens Are from Other Planets," and entirely skipped the page that listed helpful dating hints for going out with people from other solar systems. Finally, he found the page he was looking for and shoved the magazine back into Kenan's hands.

"See, right there," Kel said with a proud smile.

Kenan reluctantly looked down at the page his friend had handed him. He read it aloud: "'How to Spot an Alien.'" *This oughta be good for a laugh,* he thought to himself as he began to read.

As the boys were occupied with the magazine, an elderly customer slowly inched her way into the store. With leisurely paced movements she leaned down and picked up a basket and then, in a way that was not at all quick, she began to slowly browse, shuffling her feet inch after agonizingly slow inch.

"How to tell if someone's an alien," Kenan read. "Number One: Due to the difference in gravity between Earth and the alien home planet, aliens tend to move very slowly."

Kel nodded along, enthusiastically bobbing his chin up and down. He spotted something out of the corner of his eye and craned his head slightly over one shoulder to get a better look at it. *Oh,* he thought, *just an elderly customer moving very very slowly.* Shrugging it off as unimportant, he turned his attention back to Kenan and the magazine.

"Number Two," Kenan continued. "Due to the fact that aliens have to wear masks to appear human, and because oftentimes these masks don't fit quite right, aliens in disguise can appear to be very wrinkled."

A thought occurred to Kel. A thought that had something to do with the wrinkled customer that was slowly browsing through the cereal display. He looked at her again.

Her hair was a very distinguished sort of gray, and it was pulled back into a tight little bun behind her head. She picked up several boxes of cereal in her wrinkled little hands and scanned them, searching for the ingredients. Lines of concentration appeared across her wrinkled face.

Kel stared at her contemplating the thought that had popped into his head. *Nah*, he reasoned, *she probably doesn't know my grandma.*

"Number Three," Kenan started.

*Wait a minute!* Kel's eyes bolted open as another thought collided with his brain. Slow? Wrinkled? He turned back to face the customer, fixing her with a suspicious stare. *She's slow and wrinkled all right!* That could only mean one thing.

"Alien!" Kel cried fiercely from deep in the back of his throat. The elderly customer's head jerked up in surprise at the loud scream. She was even more surprised a second later when Kel sprinted across the store and, with a flying leap through the air, tackled her to the ground.

Kel quickly sat up on top of his alien and grabbed at her mask to reveal her for the freakish alien that she was. "Come off, mask, come off! Come off!" he grunted as he tugged even harder. The customer's pale, lined skin stretched away from her face like putty, pulling her skin tight and smooth across her old features. Her mouth stretched ridiculously off to one side as she tried to yell for help.

Kenan was stunned. He just stared for a moment at his best friend, who was now sitting on top of an elderly customer, tugging at her face and yelling, "Come off, mask, come off." It was that kind of day. Then, reality snapped back and hit him full tilt in the face. With a free hand, he pushed his mouth back closed from the slack-with-amazement position that it was hanging in and then he acted.

"Kel! Get off of the customer. Off!" Kenan chastised his friend as he rushed over, grabbed a handful of Kel, and roughly dragged him away from the downed lady.

Kel let the elderly woman's face go, and it snapped back into place with an audible rubber band–like snap.

"Kel, what are you doing?" Kenan yelled at him.

Kel looked up sheepishly from his position on the floor. "I . . . I thought she was an alien."

Kenan bit his lip; then, when that didn't seem like quite enough, he shook his arms at his sides and screamed, *"Whhhyyyyyyy??"*

The elderly customer slowly pulled herself to her feet. She stepped, with an amazing lack of speed, over to Kenan and eyed his blue apron angrily. "Do you work here?" she asked in her leathery old voice.

Kenan swallowed hard. His eyes darted guiltily from side to side. "Yes, but—" He didn't get to finish. The old lady wheeled back, then kicked him in the shin.

"Punk!" She spat the word at him from between her thin wrinkled lips, then turned and, much quicker than you would expect, she marched out of the store.

Kenan watched her go silently.

Kel, on the other hand, laughed. He clutched his belly, doubled over, and began to sob with laughter. He tried to point after the old lady, but he was laughing so hard that he seemed to have lost all muscular control. "HA! She . . ." He only managed one word at a time between his convulsions of hysteria. "She . . . she . . . called you a punk," he finally managed.

Kenan knelt down and rubbed his shin gingerly through the baggy jeans that he was wearing. It hurt. Kenan guessed that the old lady was wearing steel-tipped shoes or something.

"Whew! Man!" Kel dabbed at his eyes which had begun to tear up from laughing. "That was some funny stuff."

Kenan looked down at the *UFO Today* that was still in his hand. It was that stupid magazine's fault for putting those ridiculous ideas in Kel's head in the first place. "That does it, Kel, no more *UFO Today* for you," Kenan said sternly.

Kel tried to protest, but Kenan quickly cut him off.

"Nah, I'm serious." He began flipping through the magazine, yelling out story items at random. "No more 'My Baby's from Outer Space.'"

"But—"

"No more 'My Vacation on Venus!'"

"But—"

"No more 'Five-Thousand-Dollar Reward for Photos of Alien Life.'"

"But—"

"Five-Thousand-Dollar Reward for Photos of Alien Life!!" Kenan repeated in a different, far more interested tone of voice.

"You already said that one," Kel offered helpfully, but Kenan wasn't paying attention.

"Five thousand dollars for one picture?" Kenan peered at the article closer to make sure he wasn't reading it wrong. He wasn't.

A small smile stole its way across Kenan's face. Then, as he rubbed his hands together thoughtfully in front of him, it grew into a big smile, which soon turned itself into a devious, gleaming, scheming sort of a grin.

Kel knew that look. He had seen it a lot. And it always meant one thing.

"Kenan, what's that look for?" His voice shook nervously because he already knew the answer.

"Because, Kel," Kenan answered, "I've got a plan."

# CHAPTER THREE

Roger Rockmore was not a small man. In fact, he had probably never been called small in his entire life, unless it happened to be by someone who stood taller than the six feet four inches that Roger stood. Roger was many things—Kenan's father, a well-respected air traffic controller, bald—but small wasn't one of them. His two beefy arms sprouted out from his muscular shoulders, which sat on top of his thick barrel chest like two large round sandbags. Even his eyes were big, bulging out from underneath his shiny bald head in a way that always seemed to make him look angry or, at the very least, as if his underwear were slightly too small. No, Roger was definitely not small. He was, however, at this particular moment, green.

"Kyra, are you almost done yet?" A high-pitched whine had replaced Roger's usual booming baritone of a voice.

"Just hold still, Daddy," replied Roger's twelve-year-old daughter in her sweet high-pitched voice. Kyra impatiently squeezed more of the green, goopy face mask onto her hands and began smearing it across her father's face, being extra careful not to get any in his eyes.

Roger's evening was not at all going according to his plan. His plan had included coming home from a long and tiring day of directing air traffic from the control tower of Chicago's international airport where he worked, slumping down on the comfortable brown couch that occupied the center of the Rockmores' large, homey living room, kicking off the uncomfortable dress shoes, and catching the last half of the Bulls game on TV.

What his plan did not include was getting a facial from his youngest child. But, plan or no plan, that was what was happening.

Roger ran the events of the evening through his head once again, trying to figure out exactly where things had turned against him.

Step one: come home from work. That had happened just fine. Just the way he had expected it to. Nothing out of the ordinary there.

Step two: slump down on couch. No problem with that one. He had easily slunk his imposing frame down into the soft downy cushions of the couch, which sat just the perfect distance from the television for proper basketball viewing.

Step three: kick off uncomfortable shoes. True, he had a little difficulty with this step. From his cozy position on the couch, Roger wasn't actually able to reach his feet, and so, after several straining attempts, he at last had to resort to kicking at the heel of one shoe with the toes of his other foot, until the shoe popped off and landed on the decorative area rug at his feet. So step three hadn't gone perfect, but still, no real damage.

Step four: watch Bulls game. Ah-ha. This was where everything had fallen apart. First, he hadn't been able to find the remote. Major problem. There was no way, after all the trouble he took to properly slump, that he was going to get back up and turn the TV on. Uh-oh, his plan was unraveling. He glanced desperately from side to side hoping to find something within arm's reach that he could throw at the TV in the hopes of hitting the "on" switch.

He looked to his right. Several promising knick-knacks sat perched on a small end table just next to the curved arm of the couch. There was a lamp, but that probably wouldn't do. Several picture frames were laid out on display just underneath the lamp, each one proudly showing off pictures of the Rockmore family: Roger, his wife Sheryl, Kyra, and of course Kenan. Oddly enough, Kel had snuck his way into a few of those pictures, too. Roger frowned for a moment as he thought of Kel. It's not that Roger didn't like Kel. He liked him just fine. In fact he would have liked very much if Kel were to go far, far away and never return. Somehow, whenever Kel was around, Roger always ended up getting hurt.

He thought for a moment. Maybe he could throw one of the pictures that had Kel in it. *Nah,* he reasoned, *might hurt the TV.*

He rolled his head to the other side and continued his search. Nothing over there. True, there were a few items on the wooden dining-room table which sat just outside the swinging door that led to the kitchen, but that was way too far for Roger to reach.

Just when he was about to give up and lug his lazy body out of the couch and over to the television, Kyra skipped into the room.

Roger smiled.

"Kyra honey, can you switch on the TV for me?" he had asked in his most friendly, paternal, do-this-for-me-and-maybe-I'll-raise-your-allowance sort of way.

Kyra skipped over to him and kissed him on top of his smooth head. "Sure thing," she said; then she happily bounded over to the TV and switched it on. The deep reflective black of the screen faded into a lighter shade of gray. Then, in a way that made Roger very happy, the thousands of little dots of color that made up the TV screen flickered to life in the form of Scotty Pippen going up for the slam dunk.

"Yes!" Roger squealed excitedly. "Two points."

"Hey Daddy, can you help me with something? You won't have to move or anything," Kyra said.

That seemed fine to Roger, especially the not-having-to-move part. He was always happy to spend a little quality time with his children. And if he could go on watching the Bulls beat up on the Orlando Magic at the same time, then all the better for him.

Kyra pulled a small plastic tube out of her pocket. Roger looked at it curiously and was just able to make out the words "Pore-Cleansing Face Mask" before Kyra began squeezing some goopy green substance into her waiting hand. It was at this point that Roger's evening went horribly wrong.

* * *

Roger tried to crane his thick neck to one side in a desperate attempt to see around Kyra, who was standing directly between him and his courtside view of Michael Jordan.

"Stop fidgeting, Daddy, you're going to make me mess up," scolded Kyra. She reached out with her goop-covered hands and firmly pushed her dad's head back into place.

Roger looked deep into the eyes of his only daughter, noticing how her face still retained some of its cute little-girl roundness. Her hair poked out from the sides of her head in pigtails, just like it had when she was three. *She's growing up so fast,* Roger thought to himself, realizing that these times together wouldn't last forever. But, on the other hand, from the sound of it, he was missing quite a basketball game.

"Sheryl! Help!" he yelled, leaning his green face towards the stairs which rested quietly against the rear wall of the living room. "Sheryl, please!" His voice had a desperate, pleading tone to it.

Roger smiled hopefully as he heard the light sound of footsteps on the stairs. A moment later, his wife appeared.

"What is it, honey, what's wrong?" Sheryl asked as she quickly descended the carpeted steps, wondering why her husband had sounded so desperate and pleading. She hoped everything was okay.

"Look what your daughter is doing to me," Roger complained as he turned to look at his wife, revealing the green caked layer of face mask that covered his wide brown face. He arched his eyebrows up in a silent, begging expression.

Sheryl did not look happy. This was what her husband called her away from her evening aerobics for? She pulled her robe tightly around the leotard that she wore and tied it snugly. Her short, smart hairdo lay flat and limp against her head from the sweat of the workout. It did not look happy for Roger either.

"This is what you called me down here for?" Sheryl demanded, cocking her hips out to the side angrily.

"But, honey," he sniffed, offering a pathetic, puppy dog look at his wife, "I'm missing the game."

Sheryl's expression did not waver as she stared out at her husband slumped down across the couch and at Kyra who stood in front of him, eagerly waiting to finish the job she had started. "Kyra," she started. Roger's heart jumped. Thank goodness! Freedom!

"Don't forget to do his nails when you're done!" Before Roger could protest, she turned and marched back up the stairs.

"But . . . But . . . ," Roger sputtered as he tried to form a complete sentence.

"Don't worry, Daddy," Kyra said gleefully as she went back to the task of smearing. "You'll thank me someday. You know, youthful-looking skin doesn't come easy. And let's face it, you aren't getting any younger."

Roger opened his mouth to say something and got a mouthful of face mask. He was not having a good time.

Kenan was having a very good time. His plan was all coming together perfectly. He was so happy, in fact, that he could have hugged Kel and his beautiful and glossy UFO magazine, if such displays of affection didn't make him horribly uncomfortable. He thought, instead, that the next time Kel walked by maybe he would punch him in the arm or something.

The idea had struck him as soon as he spotted the full-color ad in *UFO Today* magazine. The ad promised five thousand dollars to anyone who could produce photographic proof of alien life. Kenan salivated at the thought of all that money. His eyes stared greedily off into the distance, and that's when it hit him. *He* could produce photographic proof of alien life. All he needed was a picture. How hard could that be? After all, he had a camera.

All that was standing between him and the five thousand dollars was the actual "alien life" part of the equation.

Kenan pondered that part intently. It's not as if he could just invite an alien over for dinner and then, in between the broiled trout amandine and the carrot cake that he had prepared for dessert, just jump up and yell "Cheese!" First of all, Kenan did not have the faintest idea of how to cook trout amandine. Secondly, that plan was doomed to failure because of the very simple fact that aliens absolutely did not exist, and therefore would be very hard to invite over for dinner.

*Well,* Kenan thought to himself, *since there are no such things as aliens, I'll just have to invent some.* And that's exactly what he set out to do.

Kenan's plan lay spread out in front of him across the oil-stained cement floor of his garage like discarded pieces of some metallic puzzle. Laying in the cluttered mess were small bits of electronic doodads mixed in with old and forgotten scraps of metal. A mound of old Christmas lights winked on and off, illuminating a small pile of discarded switches and buttons. In the center of the mess of spare parts lay Kenan's creation, the alien mothership.

He took a step back and gazed proudly at his masterpiece. The small metallic round saucer looked a little like a hubcap. More specifically, it looked a little like the remaining three hubcaps on his father's car. It would have looked a lot more like the other hubcaps except that now, glued across the protruding shelf that stuck out above the circular base of the hubcap, there were small little electronic doodads. Switches and buttons and bits of hi-tech–looking metal were intermingled with old model airplane parts across the entire exterior of the ship. The result was pretty astonishing.

It still looked like a hubcap, but now, instead of a normal hubcap, it looked like a hi-tech alien hubcap that may have traveled millions of light-years from another planet, only to land underneath the single lightbulb that hung from the roof, casting a wan yellow glow over Kenan's garage.

*Still needs something.* He glanced around the strewn pile of parts, selected the small strand of blinking Christmas lights, and wrapped them around the outer rim of the saucer. *Not bad. Not bad!* he thought as he rubbed his chin in gleeful contemplation of the five thousand dollars that gleamed so brightly in his future, like the blinking Christmas lights that danced across his eyelids.

"Hey, I got more parts and stuff." Kel burst into the garage with an armful of parts and a wide, proud grin plastered across his handsome face. "Check out all this cool stuff." Kel was having a good time. Usually Kenan's plans ended with them getting into trouble, and, more often than not, some level of personal pain was involved. But this one wasn't like that at all. This one was cool.

Kel dumped the armful of small motorized bits onto the floor in one large heap, and Kenan immediately started rummaging through them.

"Kel, these are great!" Kenan exclaimed excitedly as he fingered several very cool and hi-tech–looking electronic pieces. They looked like parts to very small motors along with little push buttons and metallic coils and bits of plastic casing. "Where did you find all this stuff?" Kenan asked absently as he separated several especially impressive pieces from the new pile and set them aside to be added to their spaceship.

"Oh, I found it all in your kitchen," Kel replied.

"Good job. Man, you found all this in my kitchen, huh?"

*Kitchen? Kitchen? Kel found all of this in my kitchen.* That seemed a little weird. Kenan didn't seem to remember any spare electronic parts lying around in his kitchen. An uncomfortable kind of sensation replaced the joyful excited feeling that had been dancing around in Kenan's belly. "Kel, where in my kitchen did you find all of this?" A worried tremble had somehow crept its way into Kenan's voice.

"Oh, you know, I found some of it in the toaster, like

that metal coil there. And a lot of it came from your mom's blender and microwave," Kel bragged. "Oh, see those handles and washers and things there? I took those off of your sink."

Kenan winced ever so slightly to himself. "So, you're saying that you took apart the appliances in the kitchen and took all of the stuff that was inside of them out and now all that stuff is laying in a big messy pile on the floor of my garage? Is that what you're saying?" Kenan asked, desperately hoping that the answer was no.

"Yeah!" Kel answered, bobbing excitedly from side to side. "Pretty smart thinking, eh? Eh?" Kel smacked Kenan lightly on the shoulder.

"Oh, man!" Kenan turned away, his face furrowed in worry. "You are gonna get me in so much trouble when my parents find out." He gnawed on his fist as he tried to think of a way out of their predicament. He gave up. "Look, let's just hurry up and take the picture. Maybe we can get all of this stuff put back before anyone notices."

Roger lifted the small slice of cucumber off of his eye. His pupil danced furtively to the right, then quickly raced across his eyeball to glance furtively to the left. No one was there. He was alone. Kyra had taped the cucumbers to his eyes with small pieces of tape that connected the small vegetable slices to his forehead. Then, she left him sitting on the couch and had headed upstairs while the mask dried. Now was his chance. He had to make a break for it.

Quickly, he pulled the pieces of cotton out from between his toes where Kyra had placed them to keep the purple, glittery toenail polish from smudging while it dried. Then, with one more leery look around, he jumped to his feet and headed for the kitchen. As soon as he was up, he lost his grip on the slimy cucumber and it slipped back down over his eye. He went to grab it again, but before he could, his foot slammed into the coffee table in front of him.

His mouth opened wide in pain, and he started to cry out as throbbing waves of agony shot up from his injured toe. He quickly stuffed his hand in his mouth and bit down on it to stifle the noise. After all, if he screamed, they would hear him and they would come. He hopped up and down on one foot until the shooting ache in his big toe subsided into a dull throb. Then, he carefully lifted the cucumber up off of his eye again and crept silently into the kitchen.

The kitchen was dark. Roger thought briefly about turning the light on but then decided against it. They might hear. He couldn't afford to take any chances if he ever wanted his skin care nightmare to end. He carefully made his way around the shadowy shapes of the kitchen table and the refrigerator which loomed up out of the darkness at him. The faint digital readout from the microwave clock bathed the counter in a dull green glow.

Finally, Roger found his way to the sink. He ran his hands over it, feeling its silvery metal coolness under his fingers. This whole terrible experience was about to end. He turned the water on and shoved his hands under the faucet.

Something was wrong. His hands weren't getting wet. Probably because no water was coming from the faucet. He scrunched his green forehead up in frustration and tried again.

He turned the handle of the sink on full, then put his hands under the nozzle. Nothing. He tried turning the handle again, then suddenly realized what the problem was. The handle was not there.

Roger frantically groped around in the dark, searching for the missing handle. *Oh, where could it be?!* Why did this always have to happen to him! Everyone was out to get him. First his daughter, then his wife, and now even the plumbing was trying to ruin his evening. Then, another thought occurred to him. Kel.

It was all making sense now. Hadn't he seen Kel rummaging around in the kitchen earlier in the evening? Yes, he was almost positive that he had. The whole diabolical plan finally came together inside Roger's burning brain. Kel had been instrumental in ruining a number of Roger's evenings, so why should one more come as any surprise? And he knew that when Kel was involved, then so was . . .

"KENAN!!!!!" he bellowed at the top of his lungs.

"A little lower," Kenan directed from behind the viewfinder on his small camera.

Kel clung tightly to the tree branch which, very politely, held him about fifteen feet over the concrete driveway below. He let a little more of the slack from the fishing line slip through his fingers, which dropped the very spacey looking hubcap, which was attached to the other end, a few feet closer to the earth.

"Kenan, aren't people gonna wonder why these aliens are so small? You know, if they can fit into a hubcap and all," Kel said from his makeshift perch above Kenan's front yard.

Kenan ignored his friend. He was too busy finding the perfect angle from which to shoot the alien landing. The night was cooperating in a way that Kenan was very thankful for. The bright full moon hung low in the darkened night sky, like a giant illuminated basketball which seemed to be floating just a few feet off of the sloping roof of the Rockmore house. A few wispy tendrils of clouds obscured small bits and pieces of the glowing orb, adding a very nice, ominous, alien-landing kind of feel to the night.

Kenan knelt down on the moist grass of his well-tended front yard. The cool night air sent shivers down his spine. *Or was that from the excitement,* he wondered. He squinted his eyes and peered through the camera's tiny viewfinder again. Perfect. He had it all—house, moon, alien spaceship. It just needed to be a little lower.

"Just a little lower," he said again.

Up on the tree trunk, a small squirrel had curiously picked its way from branch to branch to get a better view of the proceedings. It perched its small, furry brown body on a thin branch, just above the one that Kel was clinging to, and rubbed its tiny little paws together in a way that made it look like it was up to something. Then, because it was indeed up to something, it dropped an acorn onto Kel's head.

Plunk. "Owwww." Kel went to rub his head and then decided that things would probably work out better for him if, instead of rubbing his head, he continued clutching the branch for dear life. "There's a squirrel up here that's dropping acorns on my head!" he yelled down to his friend as he tried to lower the fake alien spaceship and not fall off of the branch and plummet to the ground all at the same time.

"Just ignore it and it will go away!" came Kenan's helpful reply. "Now hold it steady; it's perfect right there."

The squirrel chattered to itself in its high-pitched rodent voice. Then, it dropped another acorn.

"Owwww," Kel complained. "Kenan, I don't think this 'ignoring it' thing is working. I'm ignoring it, but it's not going away!"

"Well, ignore it harder then."

Kel shut his eyes tightly and strained with all his might to ignore the small furry squirrel that was bombarding him from above.

Three more acorns rained down on top of his head in quick succession, followed by a quick high-pitched squirrel laugh. *Oh, that does it,* thought Kel. *You're mine, squirrel.* He released his tight grip on the branch and swung his arm wildly at his taunting squirrel nemesis. "Come on, squirrel, come here and face me like a man . . . or a squirrel . . . or whatever!" Kel yelled at his cute furry adversary.

Snap! The flash illuminated the night for a brief second then the world faded back into darkness. *That was a good one,* thought Kenan. *Better take a couple more though, just to make sure they turn out.*

He reframed the shot through the viewfinder. There it was. Spaceship hovering above the house. Moon in the background, partially eclipsed by the low-lying clouds. Really angry looking guy with a green face storming towards him yelling his name. *Huh?*

"Kenan!!!" Roger bellowed, his thick, deep voice booming through the night air like a cannon shot.

*Uh-oh!* "Oh, uh . . . hi Daddy," Kenan started sheepishly. "That face is a lovely shade of green on you. Really brings out the color of your bald head. Heh-heh." Kenan laughed. Roger didn't. He just kept on coming. There was only one thing for Kenan to do.

Snap! The flash illuminated the night.

Roger threw his hands in front of his face, trying to shield himself from the blinding flash of Kenan's camera. The cucumbers mounted over his eyes slipped back in front of them. And that was the moment that Kel chose to fall out of the tree.

The squirrel had been taunting him from just out of arm's length, keeping up a dual campaign of dropping tiny, painful little acorn bombs on his head, then sitting up on its furry hind legs and laughing in its chattering rodent way. Kel had had enough. He wasn't going to take this lying down, so he stood up, and before he had time to realize what a huge mistake that was, he lost his footing, reached out in one last desperate attempt to take the squirrel with him, missed, and fell out of the tree.

SNAP, SNAP, SNAP. Kenan popped off three more shots in quick succession, creating a strobe effect which seemed to freeze Kel's plummet from the tree to Roger's head in stop-motion. Then, before the flash had a chance to recharge, Kel crashed down on top of Kenan's green-faced dad, sending them both collapsing to the ground in a heap.

"Hey, thanks for breaking my fall, Mr. Rockmore!" Kel said happily as he leapt off of Roger's back and brushed himself off.

Roger groaned. He only hoped that whatever bad thing he had done to deserve a day like today had been well worth it.

# CHAPTER FOUR

Eighteen-and-a-Half-Minute Photo sat wedged into a long, small outdoor strip of shops just in between Sally's Sausage Hut and one of the twelve Pizza Farm franchises that graced Chicago with not only "Food and Fun," but also the opportunity to have both food and fun in the company of many animals.

Eighteen-and-a-Half-Minute Photo didn't have any animals, but what it did have was a machine that would develop your photos in an astonishingly quick eighteen minutes and thirty seconds, give or take.

Inside the small, squat, flatly lit room that housed the fastest photo-processing shop in Chicago sat the very impressive, very large, very loud machine that made its existence possible—the Develop-O-Matic 3000. The Develop-O-Matic looked a lot like the disfigured offspring of a medium-sized copying machine and a large semi truck, only it was much louder than either of them.

In fact, the noise that the developer made, as it sucked in negatives from one side, processed them in its numerous tanks of fluids and solutions, and then spit them out the other side as glossy three-by-five-inch prints, was about the noise you would expect to hear from a passing jet plane if that jet plane just happened to be passing right through your head.

The long counter shook slightly with each rumbling vibration of the large, loud mechanism. On top of it, displayed stacks of film and lens paper danced slowly across the glass countertop, moving in time to the rhythm of the high-powered shakes. One of the small cylindrical rolls of film shook its way to the edge of the counter and then jumped off.

Rob Renner reached down and snatched the small container of film out of midair without even looking up from his copy of *UFO Today*. Rob Renner didn't look any different from most other photo shop employees. He was about the same height as other photo shop employees, he was about the same weight as other photo shop employees, and though his eyes were a little bluer than those of many people who worked in photo shops, they still had the same slightly glazed I've-stared-at-too-many-pictures look about them. Even the pale blue dress shirt that was neatly buttoned up to his neck and finished off with a large white name tag which read "I'm Rob" didn't really seem out of place for a photo shop employee. But Rob Renner was much more than the average photo shop employee. Much, much more.

His eyes continued to scan the article entitled "Flying Alien Brain Spotted over Newark" as he absently set the stray roll of film back on the counter.

Rob Renner had worked at the photo shop for over a

year. That was quite enough time for him to get used to a lot of things. Unfortunately, the ear-shatteringly loud noise that emanated from the mechanical bowels of the machine as it spewed out colorful prints in about the same amount of time that it would take for you to watch eighteen and a half minutes of your favorite TV show wasn't one of them. In fact, the only reason he was able to sit behind the counter, calmly reading the latest news on life from other planets, was the two small balls of cotton that he stuffed into his ears every morning before work. Unfortunately, though the cotton balls did a pretty good job of muffling the noise of the processing machine, they did a remarkable job of blocking out all other noises entirely.

"Hey! Hello! Can you hear me?!" Kenan clutched his hands tightly over his ears and screamed at the top of his lungs. The curly blond–haired man behind the counter didn't seem to hear a thing. He casually flipped the page of his *UFO Today* magazine without glancing up. Kenan decided to try again, a little louder. "Can you hear me?!!!!"

Kel casually leaned over to Kenan's ear and screamed, "Yes, I can hear you. I'm standing right here!"

Kenan's head vibrated back and forth as Kel's voice continued to painfully bounce its way around his eardrum. "I wasn't talking to you." Kenan swatted his friend on the shoulder several times to illustrate his point. "I was talking to that guy!"

"Ohhhh. I don't think he can hear you."

"Ya think?" Kenan screamed sarcastically over the din.

"Here," Kel suggested, "let me try." He inhaled deeply, puffing his chest out as he prepared to scream.

Just then, the Develop-O-Matic spit out the final print from the roll it had been noisily processing and slowly rumbled to a halt.

For a brief moment, the room was silent and still. Then, as quickly as it had come, the moment passed.

"HEEEYYY!" Kel screamed, his face flushing red from the effort. "CAN YOU HELP US?!!!!"

Kenan winced as his friend's screams thundered across the store, through the thin wall, and over into the Pizza Farm next door where several small pigs and a cow looked up curiously, wondering in their animal way who it was that was doing all of that yelling. *Humans sure are loud,* the cow thought to itself between mouthfuls of hay.

Rob Renner heard something. It sounded like somebody was standing in front of the counter, whispering to him. He glanced up from behind his magazine and was surprised to discover that somebody actually was standing in front of his counter.

Rob smiled up at his two new customers with an expression of calm and welcoming friendship. Then, as if nothing was out of the ordinary, he screamed, "HI. WELCOME TO EIGHTEEN-AND-A-HALF-MINUTE PHOTO. HOW CAN I HELP YOU?" Deep inside his ear canal, nestled comfortably against the waxy buildup surrounding his eardrum, the white puffy little ball of cotton patiently absorbed the loud volume of his scream. To him it sounded like he was talking in a perfectly normal tone of voice.

"Man, what are you shouting for?" Kenan asked, trying to be patient, but also trying not to go deaf from all the yelling.

"WHAT? WHY ARE YOU WHISPERING?" bellowed the photo shop employee in a voice that would drown out a rock concert.

Kenan cocked one eyebrow in a quizzical arc. He stared at Rob Renner, wondering silently to himself why he never met any normal people. "I am not whispering," he tried to explain. "See, you are—"

"YOU'LL HAVE TO SPEAK UP!"

Kenan looked around the small photo shop, wondering briefly if maybe he was on one of those TV shows. The kind where they have store employees do odd things like yell amazingly loudly just so they can watch the reaction of the hapless customer and laugh. He peered up into the corners of the ceiling to see if he could spot the hidden camera that would capture all the fun on film. He didn't see anything. *No such luck,* he cursed to himself. *I guess this guy's for real.* He sighed a resigned sort of sigh, then looked up at the uniformed employee, and as loud as he could possibly yell, he yelled, "WE WANT TO GET OUR FILM DEVELOPED."

"Kenan, there's no need to yell at the guy. He's just trying to do his job," Kel scolded as Kenan set the lone roll of film onto the counter in front of Rob.

Eighteen minutes and twenty-nine seconds later, the last of Kenan and Kel's photos was noisily spit out of the Develop-O-Matic's rumbling innards. It landed in a neat stack on top of the other glossy full-color prints that the boys had taken and the machine, thankfully, slowed to a silent halt.

Rob Renner grabbed a fresh picture envelope from underneath the counter, carried it back to where the photos now lay in a stack at the end of the large machine, scooped them up, and . . . stopped.

He blinked. Then, to make sure that he had actually blinked the first time, he blinked again. That time he was sure he had blinked, but still the picture in his hand looked the same. He couldn't believe it. It was amazing. No, extraordinary. No, no, that didn't quite capture the historic once-in-a-lifetime-and-he-had-been-there-to-see-it kind of feeling that leapt up from his belly and was currently doing a jig with his throat. There in his hands before him was photographic proof of alien life.

The spaceship wasn't what impressed him. Its metallic hubcaplike body hanging in the nighttime air, softly illuminated by the light of the moon that hung low and full in the sky behind it, didn't faze Rob Renner at all. He had seen his share of fake alien photos in his time. And all of them looked something like this, although the full moon was a nice touch.

What impressed Rob, what grabbed his attention and caused his brain to leap into spasms of joy, was the alien. Though the picture was slightly blurry, it was still perfectly clear that this being, this . . . thing with the green face and round buglike eyes that loomed in a fearful close-up beneath the saucer ship was definitely not human. The fact that the alien seemed to be using its vast alien powers to cause a boy to levitate in midair just above his head only helped to seal his opinion.

This was it. This was the real thing. This was what Rob Renner had waited over a year to see. And it was worth every ear-shattering day of that wait. This would—

"Uh . . . excuse me."

Something hit Rob on the shoulder. His own private reverie quickly snapped off, like a TV that had been suddenly hit with a brick. He paused for a moment, not quite sure what he was doing.

Kenan had had enough. He had waited a full eighteen minutes and thirty seconds for his photos to be developed and he was ready to go. After all, he and Kel had important business to attend to. Business that included turning over his fabulously faked photos to *UFO Today* magazine and then, if all went according to his plan, have them turn over five thousand dollars to him. After that point his plan became a little fuzzier, but it had something to do with stores and lots and lots of spending. But first, he needed his photos.

He grabbed a package of film off of the counter and cocked his arm back to throw it at the employee. He had already hit him with a box of lens cleaner, but that hadn't done the trick. Maybe this time he would just have to throw a little harder, or perhaps aim for his head.

"Hey, Kenan, check it out!"

Kel held a tiny little camera up in the air for Kenan's inspection. "It's a spy camera. Just like James Bond uses. Cool, huh? See, now you see it." He held the small credit card–sized camera between two of his fingers. "Now you don't." He flipped the minicamera into the palm of his hand and closed his fist over it, obscuring it from view.

"That's great, Kel," Kenan said with as much excitement as he could muster. He couldn't muster much.

"Look at me; I'm a spy!" Kel looked from side to side suspiciously as if other spies might, at any moment, jump out of the walls and attack him. Then, when he was sure the coast was clear, he opened his hand, grabbed the camera, and photographed the top secret "Open" sign that hung in the door. Like lightning, he snapped his fist shut again over the camera just in case anyone was having thoughts about taking it. "Man, being a spy is easy when you got a camera like this." He grinned proudly at his little camera, holding it up to his eyes for closer inspection.

FLASH! He accidentally hit the tiny little button on the flat surface of the tiny little camera and the tiny little flash exploded brilliantly right in his eyes. He stumbled backwards, surprised at both the appearance of the flash and at how amazingly bright it had been.

He stumbled back into a tall metal tripod that was set up on display behind him, tripped over it, and clumsily tumbled into a stack of camera boxes that were piled high against the wall. The boxes crashed down on top of him as he fell, dazed, to the floor.

Kenan winced. Leave it to Kel to break something. He clapped his hand over his eyes and shook his head sadly back and forth.

The employee was still staring off into space, his blue-clad back facing Kenan. He didn't move. He seemed somehow lost in thought. Kenan cocked his arm back and let the cardboard package of film fly. Bull's-eye! It smacked into Rob Renner's shoulder causing him to jump slightly, then whirl around in bafflement. He looked at Kenan with a confused stare. He looked back down at the photos and then, as if he finally put it all together, he stuffed the photos haphazardly into the plastic envelope and yelled, "HERE ARE YOUR PICTURES. HAVE A NICE DAY."

Kenan snatched the pictures, then snatched Kel from underneath the pile of boxes where he sat wearing a goofy disoriented grin, and left.

Rob Renner watched them go. He picked up the phone and jabbed the number with the end of his pen. He waited for a voice to answer. He knew the number by heart, even though, before today, he had never had a reason to dial it. He knew these things because when he started work they had told him that this was what he should do if he ever found anything. And today he had definitely found something.

The voice answered. Rob swallowed hard. He was a little nervous. His blue shirt was sticking to his back and arms where he had begun to sweat quite profusely. He cleared his throat and said with a menace that most other photo shop employees rarely manage, "I think we've got one. Go to Code Red." Rob Renner was not at all what he seemed.

The offices of *UFO Today* magazine were not at all the way Kenan had imagined them. He had pictured a large futuristic-looking building with lots of windows. He had pictured dozens of well-dressed reporters dashing about, excitedly yelling about their latest scoops. He had pictured the busy clatter of fingers on keyboards and the constant ringing of phones.

What he hadn't pictured was this. The tiny shack of a building seemed like it should've been condemned long ago. The truth is it would have been condemned long ago, but the inspector was so afraid that the building would collapse right down on top of him that he never actually managed to get inside to inspect it. And with no inspection, there could be no condemning. So the building, by some miracle, was allowed to stand.

The whole place seemed a bit off balance. The top of the building leaned wildly to one side as if allowing the other side to rest in case it might be needed later. The windows had all been boarded up long ago, and then, not quite as long ago, the boards themselves had been boarded up. In fact, to Kenan, the whole place seemed deserted.

"Nice place," Kel commented as he sized the building up and down with an approving nod.

"This can't be right. This place is a dump," Kenan replied, looking around to see if he could spot a more magazine-looking building somewhere on a nicer block. "We must have gotten off the bus at the wrong stop."

Kel thought for a moment. "Or maybe," he concluded, "this building is only cleverly disguised as a dump so that the aliens won't be able to find it."

Suddenly the door to the ramshackle building flew open and a man fell out and crashed to the dirt. He quickly scampered back to his feet and took off running away from the building as fast as he could.

Another man was standing in the run-down doorway. "That's right you better run," he yelled out of half of his mouth as the other half busily chewed on the soggy remains of a cigar that was clenched between his teeth. "And if you ever try to sell me garbage photos like that again, I'll throw you out even harder." His voice had a rough edge to it that made him sound a bit like a mobster. He dabbed at his sweaty forehead with the back of one hairy hand as he glared angrily after the fleeing man through his deep-set eyes. Then, he turned and fixed his glare on Kenan and Kel.

"What do you want?" he asked in a tone of voice that did not seem at all friendly.

"Oh . . . Uh . . . Us. Well . . . uh . . . ," Kenan stuttered, nervously rooted in place in front of the dilapidated old shack.

"Hey, you look familiar." Kel pointed at the rotund little man as he tried to figure out where he knew him from. Several possibilities ran quickly across his mind. *Dad? No. Mom? Nah, that's not it. Oh, I know. The Lunch Lady at school. No, he's not hairy enough.* He stared hard at the balding round face and sweaty matted strands of hair that were grown out long from one side and combed across the top. "Hey, Kenan," he asked, "doesn't he look familiar to you?"

"No. Not familiar. Kel. We don't know this man. Whelp, time to go." Kenan grabbed Kel by the shoulder and tugged him away.

"I've got it! I know where I know you from. Your head looks just like the pumpkin I had for Halloween last year. You know, except for that little bit of hair that you keep combing over the top so that no one can tell that you're really bald. That's why you look so familiar!"

"No, Kel!" Kenan whimpered as he tried to stop his friend from saying any more. "You're gonna get us hurt." His voice trembled with fear as visions of the two of them getting hurt danced through his head.

The man slowly advanced on them, glaring out angrily from his deep-set eyes. "What are you two doing here?" he growled.

"Oh, see . . . uh . . . what happened was, see . . ." Kenan's mind raced as he tried to think of a story to tell. Any story that ended with them not getting hurt was just fine with him. "We saw this . . . lovely building here and we just thought we'd stop to admire it and . . ."

"No we didn't, Kenan," Kel interrupted, then turned toward the round little man. "See, we took these pictures of alien life and we were just trying to bring them to *UFO Today* magazine."

The man looked at them. His expression changed slightly from one of anger to one of annoyed interest. "Really?" he asked.

"Yes," Kenan said meekly as he waited for the worst.

"Well, why didn't you say so? I'm Ernie Gills, the writer, editor, and publisher of *UFO Today*. Why don't you step into my office?" He gestured with one hairy arm towards the run-down building behind him.

Kenan stared at it skeptically. "This is your office?"

"Yeah, we like to keep our offices looking like a dump so that the aliens can't find them as easily," he explained as he led them towards the door.

"See, told ya," Kel bragged and quickly followed off after Ernie.

Kenan shook his head slowly. This was turning into one weird day.

"This is amazing." Ernie's eyes had widened themselves into slightly wider narrow slits as he peered at the photos. His jaw kept a firm grasp on the soggy remnants of the cigar. He absently blotted at his sweaty forehead with his free hand. It wasn't really hot inside, but he seemed to sweat a lot anyway. He was covered in it. Even the cheap brown suit that he wore had substantial sweat stains, which revealed themselves under his beefy armpits every time he raised his hands to gesture. To Kenan, he seemed to gesture a lot.

The inside of the run-down old building actually managed to look slightly nicer than the outside had promised. That didn't mean that it looked good. It was still a long way from good. In fact, it wasn't even in the same city as good. *Nothing a fresh coat of paint and a wrecking ball couldn't fix,* Kenan surmised as he looked around the small room that made up Ernie's office. The old wallpaper had faded and begun to peel. It now hung halfway off the wall frantically trying to muster the strength to finish the job. The brown carpet was worn in spots and an odd smell seemed to drift up from it. Or perhaps the smell was Ernie himself, who hunched over his large wooden desk like a sweaty Napoleon examining battle plans. Beads of sweat pooled up on his brow and then, in what appeared to be a desperate race to get off of his face, they ran in streams down his cheeks and fell off to land on the desk below.

Suddenly, part of the carpet moved. Kenan looked at it with a mixture of surprise and disgust before he realized that it wasn't part of the carpet at all; it was a small brown dog that had been lying in the corner.

The small dog stood, stretched, then lifted its leg.

*Well, that would explain the smell*, thought Kenan.

"Actually, *I've* got to go," Kel said as he leapt to his feet and headed for the corner which the dog had just vacated.

"Kel!" Kenan shrieked at his friend, stopping him in his tracks. "You can *go* later."

"But—"

"Later," Kenan stated again firmly.

"Fine." Kel stomped back to his chair and sat down in a huff.

Ernie Gills didn't seem to notice anything that was going on around him. He was too busy examining the photos. He was especially fond of the one that featured the spaceship, the bug-eyed alien, and the boy floating in midair. That would look particularly good on the cover of his magazine. "It's extraordinary," he commented finally.

"Nah, actually, it's an extraterrestrial," Kel corrected.

"Who is this floating in midair here?" Ernie asked, pointing to the picture.

"Oh, that's me," Kel chimed in.

"Yeah. See, the alien there, he levitated Kel up to his . . . uh . . . spaceship where they performed tests and stuff on him." Kenan had switched into salesman mode. He was gonna make sure that this guy bought his pictures.

"Really, Kenan, 'cause I don't remember any of that. See, I remember being in the tree and—"

Kenan cut him off with a sharp glare. "That's because they erased your memory before they returned you."

Ernie only half listened to their story. He was lost in thoughts of his own. Ernie had been publishing *UFO Today* out of this shack of a building for over five years, and for every one of those years, Ernie had been waiting for a photo like this. This picture would sell. He knew it. He felt it in his sweaty, round bones. He looked up from his desk and fixed Kenan and Kel with a steely glare. "All right, I'll take it," he said.

A smile broke out on Kenan's face. This was great. Everything was great. Even the pungent smell that wafted over from the corner made Kenan happy. "You mean it?" he asked just in case his ears had deceived him. "We get the five thousand dollars?"

"Sure you do. Of course you'll get five thousand dollars," Ernie said in a way that made him sound a lot like a used-car salesman that had just sold a broken-down car. "Let me just write you a check for that." He stifled a smile. These two kids actually believed he was gonna pay them five thousand dollars! What suckers!

He quickly rifled through his desk and found two long sheets of paper that were filled with typing so small and so close together that instead of individual words, the paper looked like one black blob.

"First I'll just need you two to sign these contracts

here," he said, pushing the contracts across the desk at Kenan and Kel. "Just standard stuff." He tipped a knowing wink in Kenan's direction.

Kel stared at the paper. He closed one eye and looked at it. He turned it from side to side. Nothing helped. He didn't understand a single word that was on there. "I think mine's broken," he admitted as he held the jumble of words up in front of his face as if it were a dead animal.

"You're not gonna use our names or anything, are you?" Kenan asked skeptically. "'Cause, you know, we'd like to keep it kind of hush-hush."

Ernie Gills smiled his most reassuring smile. It was the one he always used when he knew he had a sucker. "Not to worry, my boy, not to worry. It's all right there in the contract."

Kenan picked his contract up and looked over it intently. His large brown eyes scanned it knowingly. He didn't understand a single word of it, but he tried to keep an expression on his face that would make it look like he did. He ran his finger over the fine print and offered comments like "Oh, I see" or "Yes, very nice" or "Ah, I like the . . . legal stuff . . . you've done here," as he went. Deep in the back of his mind the thought popped up that he should probably have someone who actually knew what he was doing look the contract over before he signed it.

Ernie dangled a small piece of paper in front of the boys' faces. "I've got that five-thousand-dollar check right here for you. All you gotta do is sign those contracts." His voice had taken on a slick oily charm as he sensed that the deal was almost closed.

Kenan glanced at the check waving in the air in front of him. *I'm sure the contract's fine,* he thought and quickly scribbled his name across the dotted line.

Kel wasn't really sure what was going on, but if Kenan had done it, then it must be okay. He grabbed the pen from his friend and signed his own name at the bottom of his own contract.

Kenan snatched the check from the sweaty proprietor and stared at it with a glassy-eyed look of greed. This check was his future. And that future was looking a lot like a five followed by three zeros. They were going to be rich.

# CHAPTER FIVE

"What do you mean the check is no good?" Kenan's voice dripped with anxiety. His usually placid features scrunched up into an expression of worry and tension. Even his stubby dreadlocks seemed to droop a little with concern.

He stood in front of the glass window that separated him from the frumpy middle-aged bank teller on the other side. The window and the teller stood in the middle of the vast marble-columned lobby of the Second Bank of Chicago.

The teller peered down at Kenan from over the thin wire frames of her glasses. She looked at him with the disdainful look of someone who doesn't like to repeat herself but is forced to do it anyway. "As I told you the last two times you've asked," she stated in her thin nasal voice, "I mean that the check is no good. It's worthless." She turned her nose up at Kenan and shooed him away with a dismissive wave of her hand before craning her neck toward the waiting line to yell, "Next!"

The heavyset woman who was next in line dragged her chubby, cherub-faced child down the row of tellers as she stomped toward Kenan, punishing the marble-tiled floor with each thunderous step.

"But you don't understand, lady," Kenan protested to the glass partition which seemed only slightly less interested in hearing his plea than the teller behind it. "See, I sold these pictures to a magazine and that's the money they owe me. See, so that check has to be good."

The burly customer approached Kenan and stuck her free hand on her hip, all the while keeping her young son's hand swallowed up firmly in her own meaty grasp. "Hey buddy, I'm next in line here."

"Yeah, but—" Before he could finish she shoved him rudely aside and barreled her way up to the counter. Her round-faced two-year-old turned to look at Kenan. A smile lit up his little face; then he stuck his tongue out and spit.

"Why you little brat!" Kenan mouthed in surprise as the little boy put his hands to his ears and began waving them back and forth tauntingly.

Kel burst into the large high-ceilinged lobby of the bank. An excited grin was plastered across his face, and something was tightly clutched in one of his hands. He cocked his head from side to side as his eyes scanned the room for his friend.

"Keeeeennaaaaaaan!!!" he screamed in a blustery bellow from across the room. His voice echoed off of the finely decorated walls of the bank and lingered there in the cool bank air for what seemed like minutes. All work stopped as every well-dressed bank manager and bank teller and bank officer looked up from the important bank business to which they were attending. They weren't used to hearing people scream in their bank and they weren't quite sure what to make of it. The Second Bank of Chicago employees, on the whole, never screamed or shouted or spoke loudly or showed any other sign of life for that matter. They were terribly dull people that you would never want to hang out with at a party. You wouldn't have to worry about that really, because very few Second Bank of Chicago employees ever got invited to any parties. Not any worth going to anyway.

Kenan looked around embarrassed as all the eyes that were trained on Kel began to shift around to see who it was that he was yelling to. He cut his hand across his throat in the international sign of please-stop-shouting-in-the-bank. It didn't work.

"Kenan!" Kel yelled again as he started across the lobby in Kenan's direction.

He took two steps toward Kenan, then stopped, grabbed an assistant bank manager by the conservative red and navy blue tie that he wore around his neck, and pulled him close.

"Hey, Mr. Money Guy. Check it out! Me and Kenan are on the cover of a magazine." He shoved the magazine that was clutched tightly in his fist into the assistant manager's face.

Kenan saw what his friend was doing and took the appropriate actions. The appropriate actions being screaming and then bolting across the slick tile floor of the lobby and coming skidding to a halt right next to Kel.

"Kel, let the bank man go!" Kenan ordered his eager friend.

Kel released the manager's tie, causing him to stumble backwards, lose his footing, and fall to the marble floor on top of his finely tailored navy blue banker's jacket. Kel didn't seem to care. He spun quickly around to face Kenan. He had news to tell. Big news. Important news. News that was exciting enough to make him grab complete strangers by the tie and shove magazines in their faces.

"Look, Kenan, it's us!" He shoved the magazine in Kenan's face.

Kenan tried to make out what was on the cover of the rumpled magazine in Kel's hand. But it was kind of hard to tell when it was pressed right up against his nose like it was.

"We're famous," Kel continued jubilantly.

"Would you just let me see that!" Kenan said, snatching the magazine from Kel's hand in frustration. Kenan was used to not knowing what Kel was talking about, but the stress of his bad-check day was pushing him too far. He turned the magazine over in his hands and saw something that he didn't expect.

There on the cover of *UFO Today* magazine, under the headline "Abducted by Aliens," was a large, glossy full-color picture of Kenan and Kel. And right beneath that was the even bigger glossy full-color picture that Kenan had taken of a hubcap, a house, and a very mad looking green-faced man. Under that picture ran the caption in quotations, "Aliens are real. They took my friend and me and you could be next."

Kenan just stared in slack-jawed amazement. His

eyes bulged out of his head in surprise. What were he and Kel doing on the cover of a magazine? Especially one that said that they had been kidnapped by aliens. This was not supposed to happen.

"Isn't it cool?!" Kel asked gleefully, before adding a very excited "We're famous," just for fun.

Kenan stared at the picture a little longer without saying a word. A second passed. Then a minute. Then a minute and a second. Kenan's brain, which had shut down a full sixty-one seconds earlier, finally started to blink back to life.

"Kel, this is our picture."

"Yeah, cool, huh?" Kel nudged his friend with a conspiratorial nudge.

"No!" Kenan blurted out. His mind had kicked back on and was now running in full gear. "This is not cool." Then, just to make sure Kel got it, he added, "Cool this is not! Cool is not this!"

Kel frowned. He couldn't understand what Kenan was getting so upset about. He thought hard, struggling to figure it out.

"Don't worry, Kenan. It's not that bad a picture of you. I mean, you've taken a lot worse pictures than that one."

Kenan squinted at his friend. His head shook, back and forth.

"No, Kel." He was having difficulty sounding patient. Probably because he was not at all feeling patient. "I'm not upset because it's a bad picture of me," he tried to explain.

"Well, you should be. I mean it is a bad picture. It

makes your face look all puffy. And to be honest, the color of that shirt does not go well with your skin tone," Kel offered helpfully.

Kenan did not find it helpful in the least. "Would you just be quiet," he snapped. "Look, our pictures are in a magazine under the headline 'Abducted by Aliens.' Now, when people read this magazine, what do you suppose they're going to think about us?"

"That you're not very photogenic?" Kel guessed.

"Would you stop with that! People are going to think that we were kidnapped by aliens. That's what they're going to think."

Kel shook his head skeptically. "Where would they get a crazy idea like that?"

Kenan looked at Kel. He looked back down at the magazine that he was holding, then back up to his friend. Somehow Kel was not putting this all together. "I don't know. Maybe from the large headline right above our picture that says 'Abducted by Aliens'!" He shoved the magazine and its large headline back into Kel's hands.

Kel studied it intently. He stared at the picture. He perused the headline. He thought about it. He pondered it over. Then, with a look of total comprehension, he shook his head back and forth, back and forth.

Keri Weathers was not the most famous TV news reporter in Chicago. In fact, in a recent poll titled "The Most Famous TV News Reporters in Chicago," Keri Weathers's name hadn't even appeared once. But that didn't discourage Keri in the least.

She had what it took to make it to the top of the TV news game and she knew it. She had the hair, dyed just the right shade of blond. She had the teeth, power-bleached until they were so white they practically became their own light source. And she had the TV news reporter suit, sharp and bright.

But Keri had something much more important than all of those things. Something far more valuable in her pursuit of recognition and fame. Something that would get her teeth and her hair and her suit a lot more attention on the news. Keri Weathers had a story.

"Five minutes to air, Ms. Weathers," a voice called through the door to her small dressing room. This was it. Her big chance. She stood and straightened her navy blue skirt. She checked her hair and makeup in the mirror. Quietly to herself, she ran the facts of the story over and over again in her mind until she was sure that she knew them by heart. She flashed her wide bright smile at the mirror. *Perfect,* she decided with a silent nod of her head. Her teeth seemed to glow with a life of their own as she turned and confidently strutted out of her dressing room and onto the news set where she took her seat behind the desk and waited.

Kenan and Kel trudged home through the cool Chicago dusk. The sun had just begun to drift its way down behind the trees at the end of Kenan's street, and as they walked toward it their shadows stretched out long and looming behind them like elastic silhouettes that had been pulled to their breaking points.

Kenan stared, glassy-eyed, in front of him as he tried

to comprehend how things had turned out so terribly wrong.

After slapping Kel so he would stop nodding his head back and forth, the two of them had hunched down and read the article that went along with their pictures. Except for their names, the fact that they had taken the alien photo, and the description of Kenan as being boyishly handsome, not a single word of truth appeared anywhere in, on, or around the half page that made up the story.

The article told all about how Kenan and Kel, while walking home from the library late one night, were surprised to see bright lights in the sky. They became even more surprised a moment later when, out of the bank of clouds, a spaceship emerged. An alien being had descended from the ship and, using his vast alien powers, had levitated the two unwitting captives up to his unusual alien spacecraft, where they were whisked away to the alien homeworld, which, according to the story, was known as Planet Broccoli. There, the aliens imparted vast alien knowledge and wisdom (along with a large quantity of bizarre alien foods) onto the two young earthlings and then sent them back to Earth to spread the message.

It was a lie! A total fabrication! And to make matters worse, Kel had been right: the picture on the cover did make Kenan's face look puffy.

Kel kicked absently at a pebble on the side of the road and sent it skittering off into the asphalt distance.

He held the magazine in front of him, and his eyes busily scanned it as they walked. He didn't know what Kenan was so upset about. After the initial shock wore off, Kel began to think that the whole thing was kind of cool.

"Hey Kenan, did you know that the aliens told us that the secret to living forever was broccoli! Man, I don't remember any of this. My first trip out of the galaxy, and I have to go and get my memory erased." Kel shook his head at the cosmic irony of the situation.

"Kel, none of that is true. That stuff didn't happen. That Ernie guy made it all up just to sell magazines and make money. Oohhh, he makes me so angry!"

Kel thought for a moment. He was trying to reason something out. Something that had stuck in his head and wouldn't leave. "Kenan, explain to me again how come that's different from us taking fake pictures to make money."

"Because . . ." Kenan started off strongly, then petered out and paused as he tried to figure out exactly why it was different. His eyes lit up as he hit on a reason. "Because we're not trying to sell magazines. That's why. See, it's different. He's lying to sell magazines and we're not." It wasn't a very good reason, but still, it was something and he was sticking with it.

Kenan wrung his hands together in front of him. He was mad. It was one thing for Kel to be fooled; he was naïve and trusting. But Kenan should have known better. "You know what, Kel? We're gonna call Ernie up and have a little talk with him! I'll straighten this whole thing out. He can't do this to us!"

Kel glanced up from the magazine and looked over at

Kenan. "Hey, Kenan," he asked innocently, "tell me again what it is that we're so mad about?"

"Because he put our pictures in the magazine. And he made all that alien junk up. Now people are gonna read it and think that we're freaks or something," Kenan explained.

"Ohhhh, that jerk." Kel spit the words out angrily.

Kenan nodded along. "Yeah, luckily nobody reads that stupid magazine anyway." Kenan stepped up off the quiet street and into his front yard. "I mean, can you imagine if all that alien stuff got out? Our lives would be ruined!"

"Hello? *UFO Today?* Yeah, I'd like to talk to Ernie Gills please!" Kenan paced back and forth across the wood floor of his living room, the cordless phone pressed confidently against his ear. His copy of the contract was in his hand and a look of determination was plastered across his face. "Yes, I'll hold!" He cupped one hand over the receiver and turned to Kel who was resting cozily on the couch. "Now he's got someone screening his calls?" Kenan rolled his eyes. "I'm gonna take care of this whole thing right now. You just watch!" Kenan boasted.

Kel shrugged. "Okay." He sat and watched.

Kenan listened at the phone. "Hello, Mr. Gills. Yes, this is Kenan Rockmore," he blared confidently into the phone. "Yes I have seen the magazine and that's what I'm calling about." His face swelled with pride as he prepared to let the no-good magazine editor have a piece of his mind. "If you think that you can . . ." He paused and listened for a moment. "Well, I'd like to see about that." His voice had lost a trace of its confident edge. His face started to deflate like a tire that had been wired with explosives and blown up. "Oh, I guess I missed that part of the contract." He slumped down in one of the wooden kitchen chairs and covered his head with his hands. "I see. Okay bye." He dropped the phone on the floor in defeat.

"Man, you sure told him good," Kel bragged excitedly. "When you said 'Okay bye,' boooyyy you must have had him shaking. You're tough." Kel was pointing at Kenan with respect and awe. "You are tough."

"Awwwww, man," Kenan moaned. "This day could not get any worse."

A minute later Roger and Sheryl bounded down the stairs to prove him wrong.

"Six o'clock. Time to watch the news." Roger found the remote and clicked on the TV.

The distinguished anchor behind the desk was right in the middle of introducing a special report as his gray-templed face shimmered into focus on the screen. "And now for a story that's 'Out of This World,' let's go to Keri Weathers." He smiled a very soothing sort of smile, causing the worn lines around his eyes to deepen in a way that made him look like he might drop his soothing smile at any minute and instead lunge for your throat.

Before he had the chance to lunge, the image abruptly changed and Keri Weathers's face filled the screen. She smiled a dazzling smile, showing off her gleaming dental work to the home audience. Then, in a slow, measured voice she began to tell her story.

"Are we alone in the universe? It's a question that's

plagued mankind for years. Yet, tonight, there are two young men in Chicago who might be able to give us the answer. According to a new report in *UFO Today* magazine, two Chicago teens have had a close encounter of their very own."

Kenan's head rocketed up off of the table like a catapult. He stood and made his way slowly over to the TV, never once taking his wide eyes off of the screen. *She couldn't be talking about us,* he hoped desperately as Keri continued.

"These two normal high school students have not only met aliens from another planet, they actually traveled on their spaceship to pay a visit to another world."

Kenan's stomach sank. Then his heart dropped down into the space where his stomach used to be and beat against the inside of his belly in a way that was starting to make him nauseous. His brain began to boil as he watched the reporter on the news. *No! No! Please!!*

"Don't believe them?" Keri asked the unseen audience in her calm and patient voice. Her calm and patient hair gleamed radiantly in all its blond glory as she spoke. "Well, they've got the pictures to prove it."

They say that pictures tell a thousand words. The one that appeared on the TV screen that night may not have told exactly a thousand words, but it told at least twenty or thirty. And they were good ones. Those words included things like: alien, bug eyes, green, pretty moon, floating Kel, and spaceship. It was Kenan's picture.

"Hey, look!" Kel screeched, excitedly leaping from

his seat. "Our picture is on TV!" This was the best news show he had ever seen. "That's amazing!"

Kenan couldn't even find the energy to shoot Kel a look. All of his muscles seemed to have resigned their jobs and moved away to find better places to live, causing him to stand there limply. His jaw hung open, and a line of drool began to run over his lip and down his chin.

"The two boys who had this amazing experience are Chicago's own Kenan Rockmore and Kel Kimble."

Roger's mouth dropped into his lap. Sheryl's eyes bugged out of her head. Kel smiled a broad toothy smile. He really seemed to be enjoying himself. "*Whhhhy?*" yelped Kenan.

# CHAPTER SIX

A sea of reporters and photographers and interested onlookers crammed themselves into the small front room of Rigby's Grocery. Several customers that had just stopped by to pick up a carton of milk and a nice melon on their way home from work suddenly found themselves unable to leave, as they were shoved up against the deli display and the yogurt counter by the incoming hordes of spectators that suddenly packed the store.

The room was alive with scores of faces and cameras and arms and nose hairs, all gathered together in the small room for one important reason. To hear Kenan and Kel finally tell their amazing alien tale.

It had been over a week since Keri Weathers had broken the incredible story to all of Chicago. In that time the city had come alive with the buzz of alien stories and new alien sightings. The local talk shows and news programs devoted their whole hours to alien speculation, debating amongst themselves whether it was all true or just an elaborate hoax. Just as quickly as one paper would print a scathing exposé, branding Kenan and Kel as liars and frauds, Keri Weathers would go on TV calling the boys "Earth's Ambassadors to the Stars." All across the town, Kenan and Kel's pictures were plastered on everything from magazine covers to supermarket tabloids. Their names were bandied about on the local news, and across the tables at local restaurants. But so far, Kenan and Kel had said . . . nothing. They hadn't been seen; they hadn't been heard from. They had simply vanished. Until today.

"I don't know, Kenan." Kel nervously peered out through the crack in the door that separated Rigby's back room from the crowd of people in front. "There's an awful lot of people out there. I'm scared. Let's just go back to your house and lock ourselves inside again."

"We've been doing that for a week," Kenan replied as he paced across the small room that Chris used as an office. "We can't keep hiding forever."

"Yes we can. We can just order in a pizza if we get hungry and maybe we could set up a basketball net in your living room so we wouldn't get bored. Then we'd never have to leave." Kel got a faraway look in his eye as he imagined their life indoors. It didn't seem so bad.

"Oh, yeah." Kenan butted in on his fantasy. "What would you do when we ran out of orange soda?"

Kel gasped. He hadn't thought of that. Life without orange soda! His hand trembled violently at his side.

His facial muscles clenched, then relaxed, then clenched again. His internal organs began a game of musical chairs in his chest. He fought desperately to get his body under control and failed. "Awwwww man!" he sobbed. "That plan seemed perfect! Now what are we gonna do?"

Kenan walked over and patted his friend on the back reassuringly. "We've got to tell all those people the truth. It's the only way we're gonna get our lives back."

Kenan had done a lot of thinking lately about how to get his life back. He briefly considered fleeing the country but figured his parents would never let him go, especially not on a school night. They were pretty strict about that kind of stuff. Then, after long nights of flirting with ideas like having plastic surgery so that he wouldn't be recognized, he finally realized that the only way out was to tell the truth. And so, he had called a little press conference to set things straight once and for all.

An impatient murmur began to fill the crowded grocery air. The reporters and photographers that had all come to grill Kenan and Kel about their encounter with extraterrestrials were starting to get a little tired of being crammed together like they were. A thick, pungent smell hung silently over the crowd, not helping matters in the least. The polite whispers of the assembled mass gave way to a much louder, much more impatient sounding buzz.

In the back of the room, one figure remained calm.

Her face seemed calm. Her amazingly bright teeth seemed calm. Even her dyed blond hair didn't seem anxious at all.

On the other side of the room, a short, skinny newspaper reporter accidentally bumped into a much taller, more handsome TV anchor.

"Watch it buddy, you're gonna wrinkle my suit," threatened the TV anchor as he whirled on his newspaper nemesis, his patented TV smile frozen in place on his tanned face.

The newspaper reporter didn't like being pushed around. If there was one thing his years of newspaper reporting had taught him it was this: *Never let yourself get pushed around. Especially not by someone who's on TV.* He glared up at the taller man towering over him, smiled broadly, then reached out and in one lightning-quick movement, ran his hands through the other man's hair, shaking it all out of place.

The anchor freaked. "You've mussed my hair!" It was the wail of an animal in pain, or at least of an animal that had just gotten its hair messed up.

Chris Potter eyed the scene nervously from behind the relative safety of the counter. Things were starting to get a little unruly in his store. He had to try and calm these people down before things really started to get ugly. He waved his hands over his head to get everyone's attention. No one looked.

"Excuse me!" Chris climbed up onto the countertop where everyone could see him. "Excuse me!" he said again, a little louder this time. The crowd didn't seem to pay him any attention. Another shoving match broke out by the soda cooler. Things were getting ugly.

Just as Chris was about to shout again, he stepped forward, lost his footing, and fell. His arms pistoned wildly in the air as he tried to regain his balance. Then, when that didn't work, he pitched backwards off of the counter and crashed to the floor.

The room went silent. Everyone stopped their talking and their shoving and their hair mussing and stared at the pile of Chris on the floor. He had gotten their attention.

Not wanting to waste the opportunity, Chris spoke, his head jutting out painfully from somewhere beneath his legs. "Uhmm . . . Kenan and Kel will be out in just a moment," he said, trying to keep the amazing amounts of pain he was feeling out of his voice as he pulled himself weakly to his feet. He wobbled for a moment and clutched at the counter for support as the world swam before his eyes in a dizzying blur of curious faces and unpleasant smells. "But before they come out, I just have to ask one question." His voice trembled in pain. "Is there a doctor in the house?"

His hand slipped from the counter and he collapsed back to the floor unconscious.

Silence.

The crowd stared down at him for just a moment before . . .

"Bring out Kenan and Kel!" one of the reporters shouted from the back. Then a second reporter took up the call.

"Yeah, bring out Kenan and Kel."

Suddenly the room was alive with the angry and impatient yells to bring out Kenan and Kel. It was time.

Kenan sheepishly poked his head into the store, then got shoved aside as Kel burst out from the back room, eager to face the crowd.

"Remember," Kenan whispered to his friend as they made their way out to face the music, "we gotta just tell 'em the truth."

"Gotcha," Kel said, dropping a sly wink in Kenan's direction.

"Do you really expect us to believe that you met an alien," the first reporter screamed at them in a voice laced with hostility and anger.

Kenan swallowed hard. "Well, uh . . . see . . . uh . . . what happened was . . ." Kenan began to tell them the truth. That it was all a mix-up, that the picture was fake. That everything had been a big lie.

All eyes were trained on him. Flashbulbs popped off around the store as every cameraman began to snap their pictures at the same time. A flurry of hands began to scribble notes across a multitude of notebooks. Video cameras were rolling; tape recorders were recording. A mass of activity hung on Kenan's every word. Every phrase.

"This whole thing," he continued nervously, "is just a big misunderstanding."

The reporters glared at him angrily. The warm feel of hostility filled the air.

"Uh . . . see . . . Uhmm . . ." Kenan's voice dropped to almost a whisper. His stomach seized up on him.

His lungs seemed unable to draw in enough breath to allow the rest of his body to function. A nervous fire shot through his gut and went straight into his spleen as he stared out at the mass of angry faces.

"Errr . . . eeeepp . . . uhhhhh . . . we never . . . uh . . . ," he continued eloquently.

Kel stepped up beside his friend. "What Kenan's trying to say is . . . uh . . ." Kel bit at his lower lip and strained his eyes up into the air. "What Kenan was trying to say," he began, "is that we never . . . expected to meet any aliens. So imagine our surprise when we did . . . meet aliens."

The short newspaper reporter pushed his way to the front of the throng.

"So you're trying to tell us that the whole story is true?"

"Yes."

"No!" Kenan snapped out of his stupor. "No, that is not what he's saying! Not at all!" he stumbled blindly, trying to correct Kel.

"No, that's not what I'm saying," Kel picked up on Kenan's train of thought and continued where he had left off. "That story was not all true. Because, see, that particular story left out the part where me and Kenan were on the alien ship and we played games with them." Kel smiled at Kenan and offered him a slight nod as if to say, *Good cover, huh?*

Kenan stared at him, wide-eyed, as his skin began to turn a very unhealthy shade of plaid. *What is he doing?* was the thought that was pounding desperately on his brain.

"What kind of games did you play?" came the next curious query. Another volley of flashes exploded around the room, lighting up Kenan's look of sheer surprise as Kel answered the question.

"Awww, you know, Twister and Hangman and Truth or Dare."

"You played Twister with aliens from another planet," asked an incredulous reporter who never in a million years expected to ever use the words "Twister" and "alien" in the same sentence together. "Who won?" Several chuckles erupted from around the room.

Kenan's mind was numb. He knew that he had to speak, that he had to somehow stop Kel, but he couldn't seem to find the words. Finally he managed to blurt out, "No one won. That didn't happen."

Kel shot Kenan a look of surprise. What was he doing? He was ruining Kel's story. "Yes it did," he insisted, raising his eyebrows at Kenan.

"No it didn't," Kenan protested firmly.

The reporters watched every gesture and listened carefully to every syllable. This was getting very, very odd.

One of the reporters raised a pencil in the air. "Uh . . . do you have any proof of any of this?"

Kenan answered for him. "No. No we don't. Good point. We have no proof."

Keri Weathers finally piped up from her place at the very back of the store. "Yes, they do. They have the picture." This was her story, her big break, and she wasn't about to have it ruined by a pesky little thing like the truth. After all, this story had made her an overnight celebrity, and she was going to do everything in her power to keep it that way.

"That's right, we have the picture," Kel agreed, shooting a happy "thumbs up" at Keri's blond head in the back.

The other reporter tapped his pencil thoughtfully against the back of his notebook. "Yes, we've all seen the picture. But is there anything else?"

"Yeah, aren't you two just frauds?" another reporter yelled from the crowd.

Suddenly the throng turned against them. Several other reporters took up the yell of "hoax" and "fraud" and "puffy face," although that last remark seemed to be particularly directed at Kenan. Kel had to think quick. He was losing them.

"Well, you can all just see for yourselves that we're telling the truth," Kel began, "because . . . uh . . . the aliens said that they were coming back this Friday night at Kenan's house. How's that for proof?" Kel smiled proudly.

The gathered band of reporters looked at each other in a collective expression of surprise. Had the goofy, gap-toothed boy just said that? Did he really claim that there was going to be an alien landing on Friday? Yes, he had.

In one lightning-quick massed motion, the reporters turned and stormed for the door. This was a huge story, and they all rushed off to write it. After all, Friday was only a few days away.

Kenan was speechless. That had not gone at all according to plan. In fact, that had taken the plan, set it on fire, buried the ashes of it underground, and then sat on it.

He blinked twice in quick succession as his mind raced to comprehend the brand-new, utterly more horrifying mess that Kel had just gotten them into. "Kel, what was that?"

Kel smiled at his friend. He whipped his hand across his forehead. "Close one, huh?" He sounded relieved as he said it. "Don't worry, though, I think I covered for us pretty good."

"Kel, what happened to telling the truth?" Kenan asked, desperate for Kel to give an answer as to why he chose to ruin their lives a little further.

"The truth only seemed to make them angry. They were going to yell at us. See? Look how happy all those reporters are now."

It wasn't exactly the answer Kenan was looking for.

A lone figure stepped from the back of the room and made her way across the store to Kenan and Kel. She flashed her friendliest smile at the boys, causing them to squint their eyes against the almost-too-white glare that burst from her mouth.

"That was wonderful, boys," she stated in a smooth silky professional voice. "I'm Keri Weathers; you probably know me from TV."

"Hey, yeah," Kel exclaimed as he pointed a finger excitedly at Ms. Weathers, "I know you!"

Kenan hadn't been prepared for anything that had happened today, so he figured, why should this be any different. He thought things would probably work out a lot better for him if he just collapsed into a heap on the floor and just started sobbing now.

"You know," Keri continued, "I would love an exclusive interview with the two of you. Here's my card." She flicked two business cards out of her pocket in one swift motion and passed them off to the boys.

"Well, you have to say that it was all a lie," Kenan finally regained his voice. "It was all a lie," he repeated, "the picture, the story, everything. You have to tell everyone that. Please!" Kenan looked up at her with a begging expression hanging on his glazed face.

"Sorry," Keri retorted without the slightest sign of being sorry, "no can do."

"What?" Kenan exclaimed. "But why?"

Kel looked over at his friend. "Kenan, would you leave the woman alone? I'm sure she's got her reasons."

Keri nodded. "Yes, I do. I can't say that the story is a lie because I'm the one who broke the story. That would be like saying that I lied. I can't lie; I'm a reporter; people have to trust me. So, the story has to be true."

"But . . . but . . ."—Kenan's tongue seemed too big for his mouth—"it's the truth."

"The story?"

"No, that's a lie. That's the truth."

"The lie is the truth?" Now even Kel was confused.

Keri tried to calmly reassure them. "It doesn't matter. I'm going with the story anyway."

Kenan was exasperated. This wasn't going well at all.

"But it's a lie! Has the world suddenly gone crazy?" he demanded to no one in particular.

"No," Keri answered calmly, "it's always been this way."

With a resigned sigh, Kenan finally gave up, put his hands over his head, sunk down to the floor, and got on with some really serious freaking out.

# CHAPTER SEVEN

A line of cars stretched down the road and serpentined its way off into the dusky distance. It was a line of motor homes and vans and rusty old broken-down piles of metal and motor that looked as if they barely qualified as cars at all. This long automobile caravan had two things in common. First, not a single car moved. The road was a solid traffic jam of vehicles all the way back to the interstate that had carried them here from all over the country.

Second, all of the cars looked as though they had been vandalized by a rogue gang of UFO freaks. There were UFO banners and signs taped to rear windows under hastily spray-painted flying saucers. Giant model spaceships were strapped down to tie-dyed roofs as far as the eye could see. Bumper stickers sporting catchy slogans like "Aliens Rule," "Kiss Me, I'm an Abductee," and "Virginians for Venus" dotted the chrome-bumper landscape. The whole stalled parking lot of cars had come from the potato fields of Idaho and the cheese plants of Wisconsin. From the shoe factories of

Kentucky and the big malls of New Jersey where people with big hair came to buy their potatoes, their cheese, and their shoes. And they all came for one reason . . . because they were sick and tired of being laughed at.

Harold Zulowitz was particularly sick and tired of being laughed at. He had been laughed at his entire life. They had laughed at him when he thought that he could learn to talk to dogs if only he could learn their language. After several frustrating years of barking, woofing, and sniffing every stray dog he came across, he finally came to the realization that even if he did learn to talk to dogs, there wasn't a whole lot he really wanted to say. Then, after a brief period where Harold thought that his elderly neighbor was a mermaid, he finally discovered UFOs. This discovery didn't really get him laughed at any less, but at least there were a lot of other people being laughed at with him, and that was kind of nice for a change. Harold had never really had a lot of friends. Probably because, as his mother used to say, he was really, really strange. But all of that was about to change.

Harold tugged excitedly at the bushy black eyebrow that perched solidly across both eyes, looking suspiciously like it might just get up and crawl away at any moment. He stared out at the line of traffic that had slowed to a stop in front of him and he smiled. This was an exciting day. Maybe the most incredibly exciting day of his whole life. Finally, he would no longer be looked down on as a weirdo and a geek. Well, maybe he would still be looked down on a little, but at least it would be for entirely different, more fashion-related reasons. Soon, he thought, the whole world would know that Harold Zulowitz wasn't crazy. Because the aliens were coming. And he was going to be there to see them. *Thank you Kenan and Kel,* he thought.

The line of cars began to slowly inch its way forward, crawling across the blacktop highway toward its final destination.

"Hey! Get out of my yard! What are you people doing here?!" Roger shouted, sounding a little surprised at the mass of people and tents that had congregated on his lawn. In fact, Roger had gotten a lot of practice sounding surprised lately. He sounded surprised when he first saw the news story that claimed that his son had met and spoken to aliens. He sounded surprised during the press conference where Kel told the world that the aliens were coming back to land at his house on Friday. And just last night, he had managed to still sound surprised when the first in what would become a long line of UFO fanatics showed up on his lawn and decided to camp out and await the landing.

When he finally stepped out of his house this morning, he wasn't really all that surprised to find that his entire lawn, and the entire street in front of it, had been taken over by hundreds and hundreds of freaky alien fans. He wasn't that surprised but he still managed to sound like it.

Dozens of makeshift tents sprung like large unwanted weeds out of the brown dirt that had once been the green grass of the Rockmore lawn. The green grass, after hours of being stepped across and laid down on and having tents stuck into, somewhere in the night had given up and quietly died.

Winding their way in and out of the tents, dingy-aproned vendors were hawking everything from alien T-shirts to alien coffee mugs. The plastic trays that they wore around their necks held extensive collections of alien souvenirs and food, including long, thin globs of beef that were being billed as Martian Meat Mounds. In reality, Martian Meat Mounds were not from Mars. Nor, technically, were they meat. Though, to be absolutely fair, the name wasn't entirely misleading, because the food did actually come in a very unappetizing mound shape. Luckily for the vendors, reality had long ago run screaming from almost every last one of their potential customers.

"Would you people get out of my way!" Roger bellowed as a crowd of eager alien enthusiasts circled around him and began excitedly yelling questions in his direction.

"No, I am not from another planet!" he responded as he struggled to cut a path through the crowd to his car. It was a losing battle.

Harold Zulowitz was having fun. Here among this thriving pack of crazies, Harold had found a home. He had even met a girl with bright green hair that perfectly matched the color of her oversized braces, who had also spent years trying to learn the lost language of the dog. Finally, Harold fit in. *What would be nice,* Harold thought, *would be to have something to remember all of this by. A souvenir of some sort.* Harold tugged at his unibrow as he thought. Finally, he had the perfect idea.

"I've got his shirt!" Harold shouted to the crowd. He clutched his thin, sweaty palms around Roger's starched white dress shirt and held on tight. The fabric in Roger's shirt, never meant to hold the weight of a geeky alien maniac with its delicately tailored threads, pulled apart with a loud rip. Harold held the shredded remains of Roger's shirt high over his head like a trophy. Leaping in the air gleefully, he shouted, "I got it! I got the big bald one's shirt!!" Before he had much time to enjoy his souvenir, the teeming mass of the crowd, suddenly realizing that a souvenir sounded like a really good idea, descended on him like a rabid pack of bunnies on the world's last carrot.

Somewhere in the back of the crowd, a lone figure stood, somehow managing to seem out of place among a crowd of people who always seemed out of place. He eyed the wild pack of alien fans suspiciously, his darting eyes seeming to take in everything at once. He calmly observed as a pack of people descended on a guy with a really bushy eyebrow in a desperate attempt to wrestle a torn shirt from him. He didn't show a trace of emotion as that same mob, realizing that there were plenty of other souvenirs still adorning Kenan's bare-chested father, had suddenly turned their attentions towards him.

Rob Renner ran his hands through his tangled mass of blond, curly hair, then ever so casually he brought his hand down to scratch his chin, bringing the small microphone that was sewn inside of his sleeve up to his mouth in the process. He quickly glanced from side to side to make sure no one had spotted him. Then, moving his lips as close to the microphone as he could get them, he screamed, "THIS IS RENNER. THE SUBJECTS ARE STILL INSIDE! KEEP WATCHING THE BACK! OVER!!!"

Several people standing nearby stopped what they were doing and turned to see who was shouting so loudly and why. Then, after deciding amongst themselves that he was probably just some weirdo who thought that he was contacting the alien mothership, they went right back to painting signs that would welcome the alien visitors when they arrived.

Roger slammed the door shut and blockaded it with his body as he burst panting and out of breath into his living room. The remnants of his clothes hung off him in tatters. His eyes had the wild look of an animal that has just narrowly escaped being torn to pieces by a pack of much smaller, much stranger, much geekier animals. He panted heavily as he tried to slow his breathing back to normal. *That was a close one,* he told himself.

"And over here is where the aliens sat and watched TV with us." Kel backed into the room as he spoke, waving in a group of about ten onlookers all dressed in T-shirts which read "Kel's Alien Tours: They're out of this world!" in bright silvery lettering. The tourists all nodded along with rapturous interest as Kel related various alien stories that he just happened to make up right on the spot. Several of them pulled out their cameras and began snapping pictures.

Roger stared speechless, his arms; splayed out across the door to keep the crowds outside from becoming the crowds inside. A few of the more curious spectators walked up to him and snapped his picture.

"Kel," he growled in a low angry voice.

"Oh, hey, Mr. Rockmore." Kel waved a friendly greeting to Kenan's half-naked dad, then turned back to his group. "Everyone say hi to Mr. Rockmore," he said in his best tour guide voice. "You know all the aliens refer to him as the 'Big Bald One.' "

A collective "Oh" ran through the group, followed by several exclamations of "Big Bald One" before Kel waved them past him and towards the kitchen.

"Now why don't you all head through that door right there, and I'll show you where the aliens taught us their recipe for broccoli meat loaf." The group filed quickly past him, excitedly looking forward to hearing more about alien meats and loafs. Kel leaned over to Roger confidentially as they passed. "Mr. Rockmore, you might want to put on some pants," he offered with an amiable wink, then turned and followed after his group.

Roger watched them go in wide-eyed shock. He had seen a lot of surprising things in the last couple of days, but somehow Kel had still managed to surprise him. Roger was starting to hate surprises.

The warm water splashed out in friendly pulsating jets from the shower nozzle. Kenan breathed in deeply as the soothing cascade of water started to relax him. It was the first time in days that he had actually relaxed, and only part of it was due to the nice hot shower. The other, vastly more important reason was that he had finally come up with a plan. For the first time since this whole alien mess began, Kenan knew what he had to do. And this time it would work. All they had to do was to go back down to that magazine office and refuse to leave until Ernie Gills agreed to run a story admitting that he had made the whole thing up. Then, finally, this whole horrible nightmare would be over with and, even more importantly, it wouldn't seem like their fault.

Kenan stuck his face under the faucet and let the water fill his mouth before he tilted his head back to gargle. It was at this point that the door opened.

"Now right in here is Kenan. See, he was with me when we first met the aliens." Kel held the door open as the tour group filed in.

Kenan gulped down in surprise, accidentally swallowing the water down the wrong pipe. He gagged, then as if it were some bizarre form of greeting, he leaned forward and coughed a choking watery cough. He waved his hand wildly towards Kel, fretfully trying to wave off the tour as he desperately pulled the shower curtain around himself.

"Awww, look, Kenan's waving. Everyone wave to Kenan." Hands shot up and waved happily at Kenan who feebly waved back. Kel turned and led them away.

A short, hunched, elderly lady rushed back into the bathroom, snapped a quick picture of Kenan wrapped in the shower curtain, giggled in delight, then rushed off after her group.

*"Whhhhy?"* moaned Kenan.

"Bye-bye now. Come again." Kel shook his hand back and forth through the air in farewell as the last of his tour group filed out of the Rockmores' house and back into the crowded dirt field that used to be their lawn.

Kenan rushed downstairs, towel in hand, drying his hair as he straightened the jeans and T-shirt that he had quickly thrown on.

"Kel, man, what are you doing bringing a bunch of strangers into my shower? I was all naked in there!"

"Oh, that was just my tour group. See, I've been giving people tours of your house and pointing out all the places where alien stuff happened," Kel explained with a proud grin.

"Alien stuff? No alien stuff happened here! No alien stuff happened anywhere! Why must you make this worse on us?" Kenan beseeched.

Kel thought about it for a moment, then shrugged.

Kenan shook his head ponderously from side to side. "Well," he asked finally, "at least tell me how much money you made."

"Made on what?" Kel inquired, straight-faced.

"You know. On the tours. How much did you charge people to show them around?" Kenan tried to estimate the figures himself. Even Kel must have gotten at least ten bucks a head off of them. With about twenty people, that would be roughly . . .

"Heeeeyy." A lightbulb popped on over Kel's head. It wasn't a bright lightbulb but still, it was there. "That's a good idea. I could've charged all of those people. Man, that's smart thinking, Kenan. I wish I had thought of that." Kel slapped his friend on the back appreciatively.

Kenan started to breathe a little heavier. "You mean you—with the— Awwww, man!" he moaned.

"Kenan!" Sheryl's voice scolded from the top of the stairs.

Kenan winced. "Yes, Momma?"

His mother marched down the stairs as she admonished her son. "Your father is upstairs in tatters from that crowd out front. I want you to put an end to this whole thing right now!"

"Don't worry, I've got a plan. Come on, Kel."

"Where are we going?"

"We're going to the one person who can put an end to this whole thing without it all looking like it was our fault."

"Santa Claus?"

"No!"

"The tooth fairy?"

Kenan clenched his jaw. "Someone real."

Kel's eyes lit up. "Ohhhhhh! The Easter Bunny."

"No! And how is the Easter Bunny gonna let everyone know that it wasn't our fault?"

"But wasn't it all our fault?"

"Yes. But that's not the issue right now," Kenan explained. "Now, come on, Scrunchy, we've got some work to do." With one bold sweep, Kenan opened the door and began to march out.

Hands reached inside as soon as the door opened. A mass of people who had pressed themselves up against the door now began busily pressing themselves into the house.

Kenan snapped the door back shut, and immediately locked it. He thought for just a moment.

"Maybe we oughta go out the back way," he suggested.

* * *

The second-story window slid open and Kenan's friendly round face poked out of it and cautiously scanned the crowds below through the relative obscurity of the tall oak tree that stood just outside his window, its branches jutting out in all directions. There was something different about Kenan's face. Maybe it was the new confident air that he wore. (Confident Air just happened to be the name of the cologne that he had recently started to wear.) Maybe it was the firm, determined set of his jaw. Or maybe it was the curly wig and the fake mustache that he was wearing to disguise his identity.

He popped his head back into the room. "All right, it's now or never. How's your disguise coming?"

Kel's back was to Kenan as he put the finishing touches on his disguise that would allow them to sneak unnoticed down the rough brown trunk of the tree and away from Kenan's house.

"All right, just about done." Kel put his hand to his face, making some minor adjustments to his disguise, then when he was finally satisfied he turned to face Kenan. A large, proud grin lit up his face. "Eh? What do you think? Eh?" He prodded Kenan for an answer.

Kenan stared at him blankly. "Kel, where's your disguise?"

"I'm wearing it!"

Kenan started at Kel's feet and worked his gaze upward, searching for some sign of a disguise. Nothing really jumped out at him.

"Where? I don't see anything different about you at all. You look just like you always look."

"Nuh-uh, Kenan. See, I'm wearing your underwear." Kel beamed, clearly pleased with himself. "See, Kel Kimble would never wear your underwear, that's why they won't know it's me."

Kenan's face wasn't quite sure which reaction it should register first: the disgust at the thought of Kel wearing his underwear; the incredible oddity of Kel thinking that wearing the underwear of another was, in any way, a disguise; or the sheer unadulterated frustration of having to explain the first two reactions to his bizarre friend. His face finally settled on one complicated combination of all three. His left eye and nostril took disgust. Bottom lip, both ears, and an eyebrow settled on oddity, and the rest of the facial muscles either went with frustration or gave up entirely.

"Look," he snapped, grabbing a pair of old sunglasses from amidst the clutter of his dresser. "Just put these on and follow me." With that he turned, crawled out the window, grabbed hold of the nearest branch of the tree, and proceeded to shimmy his way down the thick brown trunk to the ground.

At the bottom, Kenan quickly struck a nonchalant pose as he rapidly brushed the bark dust off of his clothes. He tilted his head back up toward his window, trying to look as though he were staring thoughtfully into the sky.

"Come on, Kel. Get down here."

Kel dropped through the air like a feather would if it happened to be attached to a very large boulder. He plummeted past Kenan and proceeded to smash into the soft ground at his friend's feet with a hefty thud.

Kenan looked down at his friend, lying face down in

the deep body-shaped impression that he had pounded into the earth. "Kel, I meant climb down the tree."

"Ohhhhhh," came the reply, muffled by the dirt and grass that were firmly pressed up against Kel's mouth.

Ten minutes later their escape was complete.

They strolled purposefully down the street, away from the line of cars that stretched out of his driveway and into forever. Kenan had a cocky, confident sort of strut to his walk as he discarded the goofy mustache and wig. He was feeling good. He felt like finally he had gotten a grip on this whole situation. Finally he felt like he knew what he had to do, like there might actually be a painless way out of this mess. Oddly enough, he also felt like he was being followed.

"Hey Kel, do you feel like we're being followed?"

Kel looked thoughtfully up into the corners of his eyes, and then when he realized that the answer wasn't there he decided to chew thoughtfully on his tongue instead. That seemed to help. He did sort of feel like they were being followed. There was some vague sort of sixth sense that was pulling at the hairs on the back of his neck. Something that he couldn't put his finger on, that seemed to place his senses on alert. Maybe it had something to do with the two well-dressed men in sunglasses that were following behind them talking into their wrists.

Kenan and Kel looked at each other as these thoughts passed silently between them. They had been friends for a long time, and sometimes each knew what the other was thinking without ever saying a word.

"Are you hungry too?" Kel asked.

Kenan shook his head. "No, I think we're being followed. Look."

They both stopped and, at the same time, whirled around and gazed behind them.

The two well-dressed men saw them turn, managed to react with complete surprise, quickly stop talking into their wrists, and suddenly seem as if they were intently looking at a very scenic mound of dirt that was piled on the side of the road next to them.

Behind them, a large white unmarked van slowed to a halt, trying desperately to look as if it were driving somewhere else.

Kenan looked at Kel. Kel looked at Kenan. They shrugged, turned, and began to walk forward again. Then, without warning, they whipped back around to catch the well-dressed men talking into their wrists again.

The men froze. The van froze. Kenan and Kel smiled.

"Kel," Kenan whispered from between his teeth.

"Yeah?" Kel whispered back.

"RUN!" And with that the two of them took off down the street.

Rubber screamed against asphalt as the unmarked van leapt forward in a cloud of exhaust and sped off after the fleeing fellows. The sunglassed men broke into a sprint, quickly following in pursuit.

Kenan's feet hastily pounded the pavement, with Kel matching him stride for stride at his side as they spurted away from their unwanted entourage.

But it was no use. The van pulled in front of them; then, with a screech of brakes, it skidded to a halt across the sidewalk in front of them, blocking their path. They turned to dart off the other way, but the well-dressed men were already upon them.

The long sliding door on the side of the van slid open with a metallic rumble and out stepped Rob Renner, his curly blond hair blowing in the breeze. His blue photo shop shirt and matching name tag had been replaced with a much more official-looking navy blue jacket which was emblazoned with the letters FAOPWTTFAL in stock white letters across the back. He smiled at Kenan and Kel as the well-dressed men behind them each grabbed a shoulder in their firm viselike hooks.

"WE'VE GOT YOU AT LAST!!" he shouted way louder than necessary. Then, before their ears had a chance to recover from the unnecessary assault, Kenan and Kel were shoved up into the van and the door rumbled closed behind them, locking shut with a loud clang.

# CHAPTER EIGHT

The friendly yellow room beamed out from beneath the warm glow of the lights in a way that made the walls seem as if they were smiling cheerfully at one another across the cozy plush carpeting that lined the floor. A long mirror ran down the length of one wall. Etched into the mirror's glass were scenes of happy people frolicking through meadows and skipping through parks and tiptoeing through tulips. The whole room had the feel of the happiest waiting room on Earth. It absolutely, positively, in no way looked anything like a government interrogation room, where special secret government agencies would bring people to make them talk. But that's exactly what it was. Large, brightly colored signs written in happy, bubbly letters were strategically placed around the room, complete with slogans like "Confessing Makes You Feel Happy Inside!" and "Talk to Us, We're Nice People."

The whole room was a revolutionary new phase in the science of interrogation. It was based on the principle that, sure, you could interrogate the truth out of prisoners in a dark concrete slab of a room, locked away deep in the dank basement of a government building where no one could hear their screams, but wouldn't it be better just to be nice? Maybe, the reasoning went, people would be more likely to talk if you made them feel comfortable. Maybe if you offered the questionee a cozy seat and a warm cup of hot cocoa, he might be so grateful that he would just break down and confess to whatever it was that he had done. That was the theory. It hadn't actually been tested yet . . . until now.

Kenan and Kel sat strapped into two amazingly comfortable plush chairs that occupied the center of the room. Their hands were bound to the soft downy arms of the chairs with padded fake-fur–lined handcuffs that were designed specially to provide for optimal comfort and fashion.

Kenan strained his head around the room, trying to make some sense of what was going on. It was all so confusing. They had been abducted by a guy in a white van who somehow looked really familiar to Kenan in a way he couldn't place. He didn't think he knew anyone who drove a white van and might want to kidnap them. Then they were hauled off and strapped to really comfortable chairs in a really friendly, really nice room. It just didn't make any sense.

As Kenan pondered the peculiarities of their predicament, Kel was also thinking of something. Something very, very important. "Hey, Kenan," he asked in a voice laced with concern, "do you think they have any orange soda?"

Before Kenan could answer, the large, inviting door across the room from them slid open with a pleasant-sounding whoosh and in stepped Rob Renner flanked by the two well-dressed men from the street.

Kenan looked up at his visitors. Recognition flooded his face as he finally figured out where he knew Renner from. "Hey, you're the guy from that loud photo shop."

Renner looked at them. His eyes squinted up as if they were confused by something. "WHAT!!!!" he shouted in a way that made everyone in the room want to clutch their ears in pain. "YOU'LL HAVE TO SPEAK UP!!"

One of the well-dressed men to his side tapped Rob on the shoulder and motioned to his ear.

"OH, THAT'S RIGHT," trumpeted Rob, "I FORGOT TO TAKE THE COTTON OUT." That said, he reached up and pulled a slightly yellowed ball of cotton out from each of his ears. "Now," he resumed in a much more normal, much less painful tone of voice, "what were you saying?"

"I said," Kenan repeated, "you're the guy from the photo shop."

Kel's face lit up as he finally caught on. "Hey, yeah, I remember you. Oh, no, they got you too?!!"

Kenan shot his friend a look. "No, Kel, they didn't get him too; he's one of them."

"One of who?"

"One of . . ." Kenan stopped, thought, realized he had no idea, then turned back toward Rob. "One of who?" he asked.

"I'm part of a little-known but highly funded government agency known as the Federal Association of People Who Try to Find Alien Life. FAOPWTTFAL for short."

"Oh, that's really short." Kenan smirked sarcastically. "Good name."

"Yeah, Fowpufftal." Kel tried to pronounce it but ended up butchering it horribly. "What do you guys do?"

"Well . . . like the name says . . . we try to find alien life," Rob explained, thinking that it was already rather self-explanatory.

"Well then, what were you doing working in a photo shop?" Kenan queried.

"A lot of FAOPWTTFAL agents are stationed in photo shops across the country. You see, whenever someone gets a picture of aliens they have to have it developed somewhere. And when they do, we're waiting. I just happened to be lucky enough to be working the day the two of you came in. I'll tell you, that picture you took was amazing."

Kel beamed proudly. "Aw, thank you. You know it was tough, 'cause when the aliens first landed, you know, we didn't have a lot of time to take the pictures so—"

"Kel!" Kenan cut him off with a yell. "Would you just stop it!" He turned back to the FAOPWTTFAL agent, his round face drawn long in a particularly pleading sort of expression. "See, I can explain this whole thing. You're gonna laugh . . . really." He sort of chuckled in demonstration. Rob didn't smile. The well-dressed men next to him didn't smile. In fact, they didn't look like they planned on smiling anytime in the near future.

"Well, you know," Kenan continued, "maybe you won't laugh now but . . . someday, boy, it'll be a knee-slapper. See—"

"Just tell us about the aliens," Renner interrupted. "When they're coming back. Where they come from. Are they friendly?"

"Well, you see," Kel began before Kenan cut him off with another well-timed yell. He didn't want to give Kel the chance to make things even worse before he got to explain.

Kenan took a deep breath and began. He told the whole story, from its Video Schmideo beginnings to the discovery of the ad in *UFO Today*. He told all about faking the pictures and their meeting with the sweaty publisher of *UFO Today* magazine. He explained about the press conference and how they were going to tell the truth but got sidetracked. The whole story from start to finish was laid out before the FAOPWTTFAL agents, who seemed to soak it all in. Finally, Kenan finished.

Rob Renner didn't believe a word of it. He locked his steel blue gaze onto Kenan's own much browner eyes and held them for a moment as he tried to figure out what to do. He knew they were lying. They had to be lying. He really, really wanted them to be lying. If the alien picture was real, then Rob Renner would be up for promotion. If they were telling the truth now, Rob Renner would be headed back to Eighteen-and-a-Half-Minute Photo. He couldn't bear to go back there. He blinked thoughtfully, then trained his gaze at Kel.

"Why don't you tell us what happened," he asked firmly.

"I can't. 'Cause every time I talk he just yells at me!" Kel indicated Kenan with a pouty nod of his head.

"Kel, just tell them the truth," Kenan pleaded.

"Yes," Rob reassured him, "just tell us the truth."

Kel looked to Kenan, who nodded at him. He looked back up at Agent Renner, who also nodded at him. A look of guilt began dancing its way across his face. "It was all a lie!!!" Kel sobbed. "We faked the pictures. There was no alien! Oh, I feel all dirty." His thin body shook violently as he tearfully confessed the whole scenario to his captors.

Rob Renner took it all in. He didn't like it. Not one bit. He tugged at the curls in his hair.

"I see," he said calmly. "So, you don't wanna talk, huh?" He was sick of being lied to.

"Nah, see," Kenan protested, "we did talk. That's what we were just doing—talking. Look, I'm talking now. Hear my words." He just knew that something bad was going to happen. "Why won't anyone believe us?"

Rob stepped toward Kenan and leaned down so that his nose was only inches from Kenan's nose. "Don't worry," he said with as much menace as he could muster. He managed to muster a lot of menace. "We have ways of making you talk."

Kenan's belly clenched up tightly, as did all the muscles in his face. *Ways of making him talk?* That didn't sound good at all.

Agent Renner turned to the two well-dressed men beside him and barked out the dreaded order. "Bring me," he said with a glower, "the hot cocoa!"

This whole "nice" thing didn't seem to be working out at all.

Not every questionee that was brought in by the Federal Association of People Who Try to Find Alien Life was treated quite as nicely. After all, that program was still experimental. It had yet to be proven that nice worked any better than the old-fashioned "not nice" way. So half the people that were questioned got the new treatment and half got the old; that way the FAOPWTTFAL scientists could compare and determine which way worked better.

Several floors below where Kenan and Kel were being comfortably served a nice hot round of cocoa, deep in the dark, subterranean bowels of the FAOPWTTFAL building, Roger, Sheryl, and Kyra were getting the old-fashioned treatment.

"We know you're in on it, Rockmore, just talk," growled the agent in charge meanly into Roger's ear.

"But . . . but . . . but—" Roger blubbered hysterically. He chalked this up as another in what was becoming a frighteningly long line of days that were not going well for him.

Just around the time that Kenan and Kel were being picked up on the street and whisked off to their very comfortable room, another group of agents had been busy raiding the Rockmore house and dragging the rest of the family to this concrete slab of a room, where they had been rudely questioned for the last several hours without ever once being offered something warm to drink.

"Would you leave him alone!" Sheryl snapped at Roger's inquisitor. "He doesn't know anything. Believe me, I've lived with the man for twenty years. He truly doesn't know a thing."

"Thank you, honey!" Roger mouthed softly.

The agent in charge put his face right in front of Sheryl's. His warm breath puffed meanly against her cheeks. "You look here, lady," he started.

"No, you look here!" Sheryl was on a roll now. She was fed up. She had been taken away from her house and brought here and questioned for an hour and she had finally hit her breaking point. "I have had just about enough of you!" she berated the agent, jutting her lower lip out defiantly in his direction. "Now, you either tell us what is going on or you let us go right this instant!"

"Go, Mom!" Kyra cheered from her metal chair in the corner.

"Shush!" the agent snapped in Kyra's direction.

Sheryl's eyes sprung open wide and angry. Her head pivoted on her neck in an "Oh no you didn't" sort of way. "Don't you talk to my baby like that! Now get out of my face!" she reprimanded from her constraints.

The agent stumbled back a little surprised. This wasn't fair. He was supposed to be the one who got to be mean and yell at people. After all, he was the one who had gone to interrogation-training school for six months to prepare. There was no way this lady was qualified to be mean. He was going to go get his boss and complain. They had better send someone down here to make her stop! He pouted slightly to himself then turned and marched out of the room.

Sheryl watched the door snap shut behind the disgruntled agent. Her eyes quickly darted over to her blubbering husband. He wasn't taking this at all well.

"Kyra, honey?" she called back to her daughter, who, like the rest of them, was cuffed down to her own hard metal chair.

"Yeah, Mom?" she replied cheerfully. She was kind of enjoying this whole experience. She couldn't wait to get back to school and tell her friends about it.

"You ready to go?"

"Oh, all right," she answered, managing to sound a little disappointed.

"Okay." Sheryl curled her hand up as narrow as it would go and tried yanking it through the tight metal clamps that gripped her wrists firmly to the chair. No good. It was too tight. She gritted her teeth and tried again, pulling harder, straining against the sharp, cold metal that bound her. It was a tight fit, but finally her hand popped free on the other side. Quickly she undid the binds on her other wrist. She was free.

"Psssst. Hey, Kel?" Kenan hissed at his friend who was busily slurping down the last of his hot cocoa.

They were alone in the room for the moment. Rob

Renner and his fellow agents had retreated to come up with another plan after questioning Kenan and Kel over steaming cups of a chocolaty beverage didn't provide them with the answers that they were looking for.

"Yeah, Kenan?" Kel answered, a thick chocolate mustache perched comfortably on his upper lip. A small white marshmallow sat nestled near its center.

"They left our hands free while we drank the cocoa. I'm thinking that—"

"Oooh! Oooh! I know, you don't have to tell me. You're thinking that since they were nice enough to give us hot cocoa, maybe they're gonna give us some orange soda next."

Kenan took in a sharp breath. "No. Why do you have to make everything about orange soda?"

A glint of light gleamed brilliantly off of Kel's eye. "Because, I love orange soda!!"

Kenan shook it off. "Well, I'm really happy for you. But what I was gonna say was, wouldn't now be the perfect time to escape? What with us being alone and our hands being untied and all."

Kel thought about it for a moment. "I don't know, Kenan."

"Let me rephrase," Kenan continued. "Kel, now *would* be the perfect time to escape. So let's go!"

Kenan leapt to his feet and made his way stealthily over to the door. He pressed his face to it and listened. It sounded like a door. He cracked it open, sending a sliver of light from the hallway streaming into the room. The hallway looked clear.

"Come on, Kel!" he called back to his friend.

"Oh, all right, fine," Kel whined as he pulled his hat down tightly over his ears and joined Kenan at the door. He really wanted to wait for the orange soda. But nooooo, Kenan had to go and want to escape.

"All right, let's go," Kenan whispered excitedly as he threw the door open and dashed out into the hallway.

It was right around this moment that every alarm in the building went off.

"Run!" Kenan bellowed over the high-pitched wail of the siren. He threw himself full tilt down the hallway.

Kel thought about it, shrugged, then figured why not and sort of casually took off running after his friend.

The corridor was long and narrow. Flashing red and blue lights blared out rhythmically from every corner, making the hallway seem a little like a dance club with very bad music.

Kenan's eyes shot from side to side as he pumped his legs furiously against the floor. Then they spotted something. An elevator at the end of the hall. Could it really be this easy? He shrugged and took off toward the elevator with Kel in hot pursuit.

The elevator doors slid silently open and three uniformed FAOPWTTFAL agents stepped out on alert.

"There they are!" shouted the first of them as he spotted the fugitives.

Kenan's eyes practically burst out of his head. He

squealed a high-pitched shriek, then screeched to a halt, and with amazing dexterity, he quickly reversed directions in one quick athletic motion and began running away from the agents. That was the plan anyway. What actually happened was a little more complicated.

Kenan dug his heels into the carpet and skidded to a halt. Kel, who was not really paying attention, hadn't actually thought to stop and instead ran smack into Kenan. Kenan went down. Kel went flying. He crashed, fell back to the ground, and tumbled heels over hat-wearing head down the hallway like a human bowling ball. He rolled right into the three advancing agents, smashing them off their feet. They flew straight up into the air and then, once again proving the laws of gravity, came down again, landing in a tangled mess on the floor. Kel slowed down, made one final rotation, and rolled to a stop right inside the elevator.

Kenan jumped back to his feet as the elevator doors began to close. Immediately he took in the situation, made a quick diving leap through the air, hit the floor hard, curled up into a tight ball, and rolled between the narrowing gap in the doors before they slid shut entirely, closing the two boys safely inside.

Kenan breathed a well-deserved sigh of relief as the elevator hummed to life and began its quiet descent toward the ground.

Rob Renner leaned back in the plush swivel chair and spun to face the young agent that had just entered the room.

"Did they escape?" he asked eagerly.

The young agent gave a quick nod and then clarified the nod with, "Both of them."

"And the parents?" Rob asked.

"Yes sir. They are trying to steal one of our vans as we speak."

Rob closed his eyes and rocked gently back in the chair as he rubbed his hands together in front of him. "Perfect," he purred. Everything was working out exactly as he planned. Producing a real live alien would definitely get him that promotion he longed for. "They may not want to talk. But if we follow them, they'll lead us right to the aliens. I'm sure of it." He smiled slightly to himself and rocked back a little more in his chair. Unfortunately, he rocked back a little too far. The legs shot out from under him, the chair careened backwards, and he crashed to the floor.

The elevator doors glided open, revealing a large underground garage. Lines of white vans exactly like the one that had transported them here filled every single available parking space.

Kenan and Kel gingerly stepped out of the elevator. Their senses were on alert. In the back of his mind, Kenan was sure that they were going to step out of the elevator and into a surprise attack. But instead there was this. Nothing. The whole garage lay ominously silent.

"All right." Kenan laid out the plan. "Now all we gotta do is grab one of these vans and we are home free."

Kel didn't seem so sure of things. "There's just one problem, Kenan."

Kenan didn't see any problems and said so.

"We don't know how to drive!!!!"

It was true. Kel did have a point. But Kenan wasn't gonna let a little thing like a valid point get in the way of his plan now. "We'll just have to figure it out then, won't we?" He led the way across the parking lot to the first of the white vans.

He glanced around suspiciously one last time, then tried the handle to the sliding side door. It was unlocked. They were halfway there. Slowly he pulled the door open and . . . there was someone in there. Three someones actually. The someones screamed. Kenan screamed. Kel leapt into Kenan's arms and screamed. The three someones and Kenan and Kel screamed together. And then, as suddenly as it started, the screaming stopped.

"Kenan, is that you?" Sheryl asked as her face hung slack with amazement.

"Mom? What are you doing here?"

"Isn't it obvious?" Kel chimed in. "They're trying to steal one of these vans so that they can escape also. Duh!"

Kenan dropped Kel out of his arms, and he landed with an echoey plop on the concrete floor. He pulled Kel to his feet and the two of them crammed themselves into the large back of the van. Roger sat hunched under the steering wheel, desperately trying to pretend like he knew what he was doing.

Kenan jabbed a finger in his father's direction curiously. "What's he doing?" he asked with a trace of amusement in his voice.

Kyra piped up, "He's trying to hot-wire the car."

"Hey, I know what I'm doing," Roger complained.

"I told you, Daddy, why don't you check the glove compartment first? Maybe the key is in there," Kyra suggested to her father from the backseat.

"Kyra, they are not just going to leave a key lying around the glove compartment."

Kyra shook her head in frustration, climbed into the front passenger seat, pried open the glove compartment, and, sure enough, found the key.

Five minutes later, the white van that contained the entire Rockmore family plus Kel quickly sped away from the tall gray building that housed the headquarters of FAOPWTTFAL.

"Now when we get home, we need to put an end to this whole thing," Sheryl ordered. "We just need to tell all those people in our yard the truth."

Kenan gritted his teeth. "But see, I don't think that's such a good idea."

His mother gazed at him skeptically.

"See, if we tell those people that it was all a lie, they are going to, like, riot and trample us and wreck our house even more. You know, they won't be happy about it at all."

Roger spoke up from behind the wheel. "So you have a better idea."

Kenan did have a better idea. "As a matter of fact I do," he announced proudly. "I think we need to give those people their alien landing. We just need to make sure that it's an alien landing they'll never forget." Kenan began to get that special glint in his eye.

"Kenan, how are we gonna do that?" Kel asked nervously, hoping that Kenan wasn't about to say what he knew Kenan was about to say.

"Oh, don't worry about that." Kenan grinned. "I've got a plan!"

# CHAPTER NINE

Harold Zulowitz was excited. He was very excited. In fact, the only time he could remember ever being as excited as this was when he dreamt that someday a moment this exciting might actually happen.

He tugged at his bushy eyebrow excitedly. He stood excitedly, and then when that didn't seem like enough to do, he began to pace excitedly back and forth. He even snorted his nasal spray high up his wide nostrils in excitement. Today was the day.

Harold had been waiting for this moment for days. Actually, he had been waiting for this moment his entire life, but he had only been waiting for it camped out on the Rockmores' front lawn for a couple of days. And now, finally, it was here! It was Friday! This was the day that the aliens would land.

In the living room of the Rockmore house, hunched together behind tightly drawn shades so that no one could see in, Kenan and Kel were desperately trying to make sure that the aliens would land.

Ever since they had made it back home in the

"borrowed" FAOPWTTFAL van late last night, Kenan had been locked in his room, hard at work putting the finishing touches on his master plan. Now, finally, it was ready and the whole family had gathered together to hear it.

Kenan paced in front of the large easel that he had set up in front of the television set, turned dramatically to face his family and Kel who were huddled close together on the couch opposite him, and in low, measured tones, he began to talk.

"Now, we all know that we're in a sticky situation that calls for extreme measures."

As Kenan spoke, Kel scribbled furiously away, hunched over the small pad of paper in his lap. "Sticky," he said aloud as he wrote.

Kenan stopped in midpace and looked at Kel. "Kel?" he asked uncertainly. "What are you doing?"

Kel lifted his face up from the paper. "Oh, you know, I don't want to miss anything so I'm taking notes."

Kenan's lip curled up slightly over his teeth as he started to say something like "Why?" Then he stopped and thought better of it. "That's a good idea, Kel, you just go right on taking notes." He tipped his head in an approving nod at his friend and continued.

"That brings us to our second option. We could just wait until tomorrow. Maybe if no alien lands tonight, all these people will just forget about it and go away." Kenan paused for dramatic effect before answering himself with, "But I don't think so. You've seen the people out there on our lawn. Do they really look like they have anything better to do than just sit around and wait forever?"

The whole family had to admit that Kenan had a point. They continued staring in rapturous attention. Except for Kyra who wasn't really paying attention at all. At least not to Kenan; she was, however, paying a lot of attention to Kel as she stared lovingly at him.

"Kyra, pay attention," her brother snapped at her.

"I am," she replied, never taking her eyes off of the object of her love. "I'm paying attention to Kel. Isn't he beautiful?"

Kenan's face scrunched up in disgust. "Eeewwww." He shook his head violently from side to side as he said it. That about summed up what he thought about Kel's beauty. Kenan's eyes quickly darted around the room as he tried to regain his place.

"Oh, yeah, so that brings us to option three, my plan. Now my plan is—"

Kel interrupted with an apologetic look. "Uh, Kenan?"

"Yes!" he replied, a little frustrated at the interruption.

"Can you start all over again? I kind of forgot to sharpen my pencil first." Kel held up the brand-new pencil that he had been using. Where the point should have been was just a flat leadless stub. Kel grinned sheepishly up at his friend and shrugged innocently.

"Would you just give me that!" Kenan exclaimed, snatching the pencil out of Kel's hand in one quick motion and tossing it aside.

"My pencil!" Kel screeched in panic.

"You're so cute when you're angry," Kyra said as she lovingly stroked Kel's cheek.

Kenan was getting fed up. He had a plan to explain

and time was running out. "Would you two stop it? Now listen up. The only way we're going to get that mass of freaks off of our lawn is if they see their alien landing. And if the aliens tell them to leave us alone. That's the only thing those weirdos are gonna listen to."

Sheryl piped in, "I'm almost afraid to ask but how do you propose we do that?"

Kenan held up a calming hand. "I'll get to that," he said. "But first, we need an alien." Kenan turned and stared at Roger. Sheryl turned and stared at Roger. Even Kyra stopped staring at Kel for a moment and turned to stare at Roger. Kel, on the other hand, stared straight off into space. "Man, where are we gonna find an alien?!" Kel wondered aloud, throwing his hands down in defeat.

"Kel?" Kenan pointed over at his father. "He will be the alien."

Roger had heard enough. "Oh, no! No way!" he protested, pushing himself up from the couch. "I've had enough!" He held his hands emphatically out in front of his body as if trying to push Kenan's plan away.

Kenan placed his hand on his dad's shoulder. "Dad," he said soothingly, "if you want your yard back, it's the only way."

Roger stomped his feet on the floor loudly. "Awww, man!" he finally relented. Kenan gently eased him back down on his couch, flipped over the first diagram on the easel, and laid out the rest of his plan.

Seven o'clock. The air around the Rockmore house seemed to thicken and darken as the sun began to dissolve into an orange stain on the horizon. The air had also taken on an excited buzz, a palpable hum of energy and expectation and completely misplaced excitement which rose up from the thick crowds below like waves of heat off a fat man's belly at the beach.

Thousands of pairs of glasses—horn-rimmed and bifocalled and tinted lenses, perched on thousands of pairs of eyes—all trained their gaze upwards into the heavens as the bright orange sun, like a four-day-old helium balloon that's lost its ability to float, slipped softly behind the horizon. Stars came into view through the darkening gray sky, twinkling like fireflies lost in the firmament. It was truly a beautiful sunset. An exquisite sunset. An amazing soul-filling vision of splendor. And not a single person in the entire vast multitude of the crowd seemed to care.

Harold Zulowitz yawned. He had seen a million sunsets and a billion stars, and quite honestly, he couldn't have cared less about this one. He, like his bizarre compatriots, was here for one reason and one reason only and it certainly didn't have anything to do with how pretty the stinking sunset was! He was here to see aliens.

He squinted his eyes up at the darkening nighttime sky and eagerly waited and waited and . . .

A low rumbling noise seemed to come from out of nowhere. Louder and louder it grew until it felt as if the air itself were shaking. Every neck shot upwards. Every eye scanned the sky. Every hand trembled in nervous anticipation. Every . . .

FLASH! Suddenly the whole lawn exploded in a burst of white light as if someone had switched on a powerful spotlight in the sky. The stars vanished as the blinding glow from above beat down across the lawn like a giant flashlight powered by a million batteries. It was very, very bright.

Harold threw his hands over his eyes to shield them from the glare as people to his right and left did the same. He dropped to the ground in excitement. This was it! They were here! His breathing sped up by about a thousand percent as the adrenaline charge hit his body like a pack of burly rhinoceroses on a mad rush across his skull. He had never been this excited in his whole life. He breathed in twice, sharply, clutched his tuft of an eyebrow firmly in his hands, and then, very excitedly, passed out.

Up on the Rockmores' pleasantly sloping roof, the large bowl-shaped spotlight sat crudely strapped to the chimney with what looked like several pairs of a large man's pants knotted together into a makeshift rope. Kenan trained the large beam of the spotlight down on the gathered throngs below. His other hand strained to reach the volume control of the stereo to continue turning up the loud rumbling noise that he had recorded earlier using a handheld microphone and the blender.

This was part one of Kenan's plan and it was a very crucial one. It involved momentarily blinding the crowds below with the large, amazingly bright spare spotlight that Kenan's dad had temporarily borrowed from a supply shed at the airport where he worked. Kenan figured if the light was bright enough to lead planes into the airport from miles away, then it'd probably be bright enough for his purposes. Besides, the airport had other spotlights there on the runway, so it's not like they would really miss this one.

Overhead, a jumbo jet roared by, the pilots carving a zigzagging path through the nighttime sky as they desperately wondered why they couldn't seem to find the Chicago airport.

"I finished putting Daddy's face mask on," Kyra excitedly called from the bedroom window to Kenan's right.

*Perfect,* thought Kenan. *Stage two seems to be coming along.*

"Great! Send him out!" Kenan called back to her.

A second later, after the brief sound of an argument followed by a little whining from Roger, he appeared at Kenan's side, tightly hugging the roof in fear.

Kenan looked him over with a curt approving nod. His face was green, cucumbers were over the eyes, and Kyra had even added a few alien makeup effects of her own—patterns of colorful lines now crisscrossed his bald head like a lipstick spiderweb. It was a nice touch. Even the slightly spacey silver outfit that Kenan's mom had quickly stitched together didn't look half bad. Especially with the bright spotlight blinding the people below, they just might buy Roger as an alien. *This just might work!* he thought with a warm twinge of surprise.

"Kenan, I don't know about this," Roger's voice quivered in fear as he huddled his large, imposing frame up into a tight little ball against the shingles. "You know how I feel about heights and all. I'm not sure I can do this."

Kenan put on his most calm and reassuring tone of

voice. "Don't worry Daddy, you'll be fine. All we're going to do is lower you two stories off of the roof and onto the ground. What could possibly go wrong?"

Roger thought about it. It seemed to him that a lot could go wrong and he didn't hesitate to say so.

"Nonsense," Kenan assured him with a wave of his hand. "Look, all you need to do is remember your lines. Do you remember them?"

Roger's speech was the third, and perhaps most important, stage of the plan. It was the part where the alien would tell all the gathered masses below that the only way to prevent the great alien attack that was coming was to go home and leave the Rockmores alone. Kenan realized that this speech made little sense. After all, why in the world would aliens alter their long-standing military goals just because a group of weirdos stopped camping out in the yard of some random family? No, the speech was a little far-fetched. But then so was driving all the way across the country to try and witness aliens from another planet landing at a home in suburban Chicago. Kenan pretty much figured that these people would buy just about anything.

Roger mumbled the lines that Kenan had written over and over to himself a few times until he felt ready. Actually, "ready" wasn't exactly the word he would have used to describe how he was feeling at the moment. If asked, Roger would probably have picked a word more along the lines of "panicked" or "afraid" or "really not wanting to do this." What he did want, however, was all these people off of his lawn, out of his house, and out of his life. And if this was what it took, then he would do it. That was the only thought that kept him going. That and the fact that Sheryl had threatened to make his life miserable if he didn't get all these people to go away soon.

"Let's just get this over with," Roger admonished. "Quickly!"

Kenan gave a sharp nod and a short salute to his green-faced alien-headed dad, then looped the thick rope that would lower him to the waiting crowd below under his arms and retreated along the length of the braided twine back through the window and into his bedroom, where Kel was waiting to help him lower his father off the roof.

Harold blinked. He breathed in, inhaling a mouthful of dead grass and dirt in the process, then coughed loudly, hacking the debris back out of his mouth. He lifted his narrow face up out of the dirt and rubbed groggily at his temples. His muddled brain struggled to try and make some kind of coherent sense out of his surroundings as it slowly swam out of the deep, sticky bog of unconsciousness that had enveloped it.

*Let's see,* reasoned his brain, *there's lots of people around so we're probably not in bed.* That seemed fairly obvious. His brain started to become a little more confident. *Hmmmm. There's a really, really bright light in the sky. Wonder what that could be.* Harold's brain stumbled over that one, then couldn't think of a good reason and decided to skip it. *Well, whatever that light is, there seems to be some kind of person floating down out of it.* Suddenly Harold's brain snapped to attention. He leapt to his feet in wide-eyed wonder and he pointed into the glowing night air.

"It's an alien!" he screamed.

The short guy next to him turned and, with a dismayed shake of his head, said, "Duuuhhhhhh! Where have you been?"

The large, imposing figure emerged from the bright light as a shadow and began slowly descending toward the earth, gently swaying back and forth on the winds.

Keri Weathers's mouth hung wide open in various stages of shock and disbelief. She hadn't expected to see this. She never really believed that Kenan and Kel's goofy alien story was true; it was just a story. Just a way for her to get noticed. She had expected to come here and report that no aliens had shown up, but that they probably had a really good reason why they couldn't. Perhaps some other important alien business they had to attend to or something. She wasn't really sure about that part; she was really just planning on making it up on the spot. But this. This was unexpected.

She caught herself reacting like a human being and quickly snapped back into reporter mode. Expected or not, this was happening. There was some really big thing coming down out of that really bright light in the sky and she was going to report on it. She quickly grabbed her stunned cameraman by the arm and dragged him through the crowd, elbowing her way through the rapturous throngs of believers until she reached the spot where the alien seemed like he would land. None of the other news services in town had taken this story seriously enough to even send a crew. So if an alien was going to land here tonight, Keri was going to have the exclusive interview. She primed her smile. She prepped her hair with an experienced hand and she signaled for her cameraman to roll.

Kenan strained hard, feet propped against the windowsill, teeth gritting from the strain. Beads of sweat popped out here and there across his forehead as he slowly let the rope slip hand over hand towards the ground.

Behind him, Kel was doing the same. Together the two of them were agonizingly managing to lower Roger toward the crowds.

Outside, dangling in the nighttime chill, Roger closed his eyes tightly behind the large slices of cucumber that were taped over them as he gently swayed back and forth through the night. He was counting the feet, the inches, even the centimeters until his feet touched the sweet ground.

Kel was getting tired. All this holding and tugging and slowly releasing with the rope was wearing him out.

"Man, your daddy's heavy," Kel complained. "He should go on a diet or something!"

Something caught Kel's attention out of the corner of his eye as he put his whole weight back, countering the other end of the taut rope that stretched out the window. He craned his neck feverishly toward it. It was something orangy. Something bottle-shaped and orangy. Kel's eyes sprung open wide with a thirsty thrill. It was the bottle of orange soda that he had been drinking before they started lowering Kenan's dad. He stared at it hard and could still make out about a quarter-of-a-bottle's worth of soda comfortably nestled behind the bright orange label. It was there waiting for him. That was what he needed. A little orange soda would sure make all this work a little easier. He craned one arm toward it while he clutched the rope even tighter in the other hand. It was so close. Could he reach it? Not quite; his fingertips fell just a few inches short of their sweet orange prize.

He tried again, strenuously stretching his limb to its limit. His fingers scraped the soft paper label. He was so close. He tried to will it a few inches closer using just the power of his mind. Unfortunately, Kel vastly overrated the power of his mind and the bottle, in a defying act of inanimateness, didn't move.

If he could just let go of the rope for a second, he could reach it. Then he would just grab the rope again really quick. He wouldn't even have to let go for a second. A half second would probably be all the time he needed. He was sure Kenan could handle the rope himself for a measly half a second. And then if Kenan wanted to rest for a half second or so, Kel would gladly return the favor. His mind was made up.

"Hold the rope for a second, Kenan, I'll be right back." And with that, he let go.

Before he even had time to reach for the orange soda, Roger's full weight bore down on the rope and Kenan was roughly yanked out of the window.

Kel watched his friend as he flew out of the window with a loud scream. "Ooops." He shrugged guiltily, then figured, what the heck, grabbed the bottle of orange soda, and began drinking.

Keri looked up as the alien figure got closer; then something seemed to happen: instead of slowly descending, the shadowy shape now seemed to be more like plummeting. She tried to dive out of the way as the green-faced thing fell from the sky but she was too late. Roger crashed down with a screaming yell on top of the reporter.

Roger stared up into the sky from his position on the ground and was surprised to find that the sky looked a lot like Kenan. Before he had time to realize why the sky looked like Kenan, Kenan fell straight toward him and landed right on top of the pile.

The air rushed out of Roger's lungs as his son rolled off the heap and landed on the ground. He rubbed at his face absently, and wondered briefly why there was green goop on his hands.

"Hey, this guy's not an alien!" Harold screamed from the crowd. "Look, that green goop on his face came off in his hands. And there's a rope attached to him! This is all a fake."

Kenan groggily pulled himself to his feet to find an angry crowd led by Harold pointing straight at him.

"That's the guy that did it!" Harold screamed incitingly to the crowd. "Let's get him!"

Kenan let out a loud screech of surprise, then took off running as a mass of wronged UFO fans took off after him like a huge geeky wave and chased him off into the night.

*Well, at least they're not on my lawn anymore,* Roger thought to himself as he struggled to remove his limbs from the downed reporter underneath him.

Just as he half stumbled to his knees, a voice rang out of the darkness. "There's the alien! Get him!"

Before he had time to react, they were on him. Rob

Renner and a host of FAOPWTTFAL agents descended on him like flies on a big bald lightbulb. A net landed over his head and he was yanked back to the ground.

"Aaahhhhhh!" was all Roger could manage as the crack team of agents began to drag him away.

"Good work, men," Rob complimented his crew. "The scientists will be happy to get a look at this specimen."

"KEEEENNAAAAANNNNN!" Roger bellowed into the night as the federal agents bundled him into their van and sped off into the distance.

Up in Kenan's room, Kel happily shook the last few drops of orange soda into his mouth. He tossed the bottle aside, walked to the window, and looked down.

"Huh." He shrugged curiously to himself. "I wonder where everyone went?"

# CLOSE

"Thank you! On behalf of myself, Kenan."

"And me, Kel!"

"We hope that you all enjoyed our fine booky adventure!"

"Uh . . . Kenan?"

"Yeah, Kel, what is it?"

"Did you ever get your daddy back from the FAOPWTTFAL scientists?"

"Yes. Actually we did. Luckily they only performed a few minor experiments on him before they realized that he wasn't really an alien. Strange thing though, now whenever he hears a bell ring he jumps up on the nearest table and shouts, 'I am Zoltar from the planet Plith.' "

"That's downright peculiar."

"Tell me about it."

"Well, at least you finally managed to get all those people to stop camping out on your lawn."

"Yeah, lucky for me, those alien people run really, really slow. And hey, who knows, maybe someday all the people in Chicago will stop pointing at me and calling me alien boy."

"I don't know, Kenan, alien boy does seem to really fit you."

"You know what, Kel. I just had an idea."

"Uh-oh."

"I know how we can get people to stop making fun of us and get to sail on a pirate ship in the process."

"You do?"

"Yep, now go grab an eye patch, a box of breath mints, and fourteen chipmunks and meet me at the harbor. Now come on, Ahab!"

"Kenan? I'm afraid of chipmunks! Kenan, why do we need breath mints? Does my breath smell bad? Kenan? Didn't this book teach you anything? Kenan? Awwwww, here it goes!!"

# About the Author

STEVE HOLLAND currently resides in Los Angeles with his wife, Hannah. He has written for several Nickelodeon shows, including *Kenan & Kel* and *All That*. He is also the author of the book *All That: Fresh Out of the Box*.